A SHIFTER'S SALVATION

PALE MOONLIGHT BOOK 6

MARIE JOHNSTON

She's used to rescuing strays and injured animals, but she's not prepared for the wolf-shifter passed out in her ditch.

Patience doesn't always live up to her name and she wants the guy she brought home to sleep one off *gone*. She's figured out what he is, and since she's human and shouldn't know his kind exists, she's worried he'll start asking all the wrong questions. Because that's not the only secret she's hiding. The sooner her stray gets going the better.

Malcolm was lost in so many ways when Patience woke him up in that cold ditch. Just when he's ready dust himself off and go back to work finding his long-lost sister, he realizes the pretty human knows more than she's letting on. Since his job to is to protect shifter-kind, it's a handy excuse to hang around.

It's hard keeping her private life private when Malcolm ingratiates himself so seamlessly into every part of it, and even worse when she likes it. But when their pasts clash with their present and her secret rescue work is exposed, danger claws at her doorstep. Will that be when Malcolm finally leaves her for good?

CHAPTER 1

There weren't many times Patience Montgomery was grateful she struck out in the love department with her horrendous online dating experiences and went to bed alone every night. But those times she did feel grateful happened when she was at work.

With a sigh, she pushed her mouse-brown hair off her face and regarded the sleeping children in front of her. Their mom, Mina, was pacing the room, ping-ponging off the walls. She had wrapped one arm around herself and was punctuating her murmurings with her other hand, talking to herself as much as Patience.

"I should go back. It's early yet. He might not know we're gone." Spin and mutter.

Patience steeled herself against the growing desperation in Mina's voice. It was midmorning, and she'd been here all night with a client. Mina fled her abusive husband for hopefully the last time, and it was Patience's job to help provide the food and shelter until Mina could do it herself.

But as each minute stretched by, she was afraid it was a losing battle. Mina had left her husband two other times, and each time she returned, she paid dearly for it. Last night was another breaking point, and she packed up her five- and four-year-old girls and carted them away before her spouse returned from the bar he got stupid drunk at each night before returning home in a rage and taking it out on his family.

"Mina, give yourself the gift of time. We're here to help you. The girls are exhausted, and you've been through a major change." Patience wasn't a therapist, had no extra education beyond her high school degree, but she'd been part of this center since before she could walk. It was a family legacy, giving her plenty of experience and knowledge.

She also didn't have a family waiting for her at home, so her coworkers were more than happy to drop the late-night cases on her. After so many years, she was used to the routine and could figure out what to say to the women seeking assistance fleeing bad situations.

"I gotta go back. I gotta—"

The employee entrance squeaked open. Patience wasn't concerned. Only a person with a key card could get in. But from the way Mina jumped, her paranoia was only continuing to build.

"Oh, Patience. Good morning." Kalli, one of the counselors arrived, an hour late, but Patience's coworkers never cared whether Patience had just pulled a twenty-four-hour shift or not. Kalli grinned and swept down the hall to the guest room their clients often stayed in, the welcoming in her eyes instantly stalling Mina's pacing. "We have a guest." Her gaze swept over the kids. "And look at them. Passed out. Good, good. It'll give us time to talk."

They'd worked together for so long, they each knew what to do. Patience didn't need to hand off notes or update Kalli on Mina's growing need to run back to her husband. Kalli read the room.

Patience slipped out while Kalli chattered non-stop with Mina, calming and distracting her at the same time.

Fatigue swamped her. She shuffled to her locker and grabbed her empty lunch bag. Her stomach roared to life, reminding her that she hadn't eaten since lunch yesterday. She skipped looking at herself in the mirror. Her otherwise plain-Jane appearance would be wan and pale with a nice set of rings under her eyes, much like the baby raccoon she helped after its mama got hit by a car last summer.

After a twenty-four-hour shift, she empathized a lot more with that raccoon. Her body ached and she wanted nothing more than to sleep the world away.

She shut her locker and bumped into her boss.

Jacob stayed out of sight and managed the back end of everything, leaving his employees to be the face of the shelter. As her older brother, he'd been involved with New Horizons Center longer than her.

"Jacob, geez. I'm so tired I thought I was seeing things."

"Go get some rest," he said quietly. He'd probably overheard some of the conversations with Mina. A male voice might startle her, so Jacob would stay in his office until she was settled. "Have a good weekend."

"Will do, boss." It was Friday and she had Mondays off. That gave her several days to binge watch some *Outlander*. She lifted her chin toward the hallway that would take him to Mina. "She's a boomerang." She didn't say it snidely, and she wouldn't use the term around her workers, but she and Jacob had adopted their own system for those they helped. One- or two-word descriptions that said everything.

He nodded. "I remember from the last time. All we can do is be there for her. Is the list of open apartments updated?"

If he could get Mina settled in one before she loaded her kids and ran back, she'd have a better chance of staying away.

"Yes, but I think she'd do better staying in-house for a

night." They kept a room with a kitchenette ready for emergencies like this.

"We'll take care of her. Go home and get some rest."

And some food.

Patience crawled into her car, and zipped through the only fast-food drive-thru in town and snagged some breakfast burritos. Waiting until she hit the dirt roads that took her deeper into the trees of northern Minnesota, she opened the first one. She'd never recommend distracted driving, but no one used these roads regularly except her and her few neighbors. And, well, she didn't have to worry about them.

A piece of sausage rolled out and onto her shirt, leaving a greasy splatter.

"Shit." She dabbed at it, but it'd be another top to add to her collection for an Oxi-Clean spot treatment.

If she had a superpower, it'd be spilling food on herself.

She bit off a huge bite and maneuvered a curve with one hand, easing up on her speed. Her house would come into sight soon and she'd finally have her long weekend.

Swallowing, she ripped off another mouthful.

Were you raised by wolves? her grandma used to tease.

If only.

Tossing the wrapper onto the passenger seat, she handled another curve. Her little cottage peeked out between the trees and her body went soft. One more burrito and she'd be tucked into bed, succumbing to sleep with no alarm in sight.

A lumpy bundle in the ditch captured her attention. She was past it before she braked. Frowning, she peered in the rearview mirror and waited for the dust cloud to settle.

Still there.

What was it? Too large to be a dog. Maybe a bear? A garbage bag? It wouldn't be the first time some idiot tried getting rid of their trash on the side of a rural road.

Squinting, she couldn't make out what it was, but she swore part of the blue appeared to be denim material.

No. It couldn't be a person.

And with her neighbors... They wouldn't be unconscious in her ditch. It wasn't like them. Looking around, she couldn't see a motorcycle or anything that suggested an automobile wreckage of any sort.

She ran her tongue along her teeth. Good thing she fueled up. Someone had to check this lump out.

She stepped out of her car and blinked in the sunlight. It was a cool day, typical for late spring. Dirty snow was still piled in the ditches, but it'd been a mild winter, and whatever the bundle was hadn't landed in more than dried grasses.

"Hello?" She inched closer to the edge of the road. If it was garbage, please be old rags. Something that didn't ooze. Picking up other people's trash was full of icky surprises.

The lump didn't move.

"Garbage dumpers," she muttered and crept closer. A mop of rich brown hair caught her gaze. She paused. "Shit."

The pile wasn't small. And it had hair.

Her heart rate kicked up. A person. But there was no vehicle around. Was he dumped?

She knew it was a he because of the size. Not that women couldn't be that big. But this was definitely a guy. Because the more she studied him, the better able she could make out that he was on his side and had incredibly broad shoulders.

"Excuse me?" she said, sounding more timid than she cared to.

No movement.

"Sir?" She took a step closer.

No response.

She closed the distance between them and stood over him. His shoulders moved in time with his steady breathing. Good, he was alive at least. Before she could wonder about

5

her personal safety, she crouched as far away as possible but close enough to reach out and nudge one heavily muscled arm. "Hey?"

Nothing.

Circling him, she had a dying need to know what he looked like. If she was getting taken down by a stranger, she wanted to see his face.

Admittedly, this stranger didn't seem like he'd attack anyone any time soon.

A leather coat flap obscured his face. Since he was breathing, she pushed him to his back. A normal person would call an ambulance, but there was no way she'd risk that. With her luck, Damian would be on duty, and she couldn't risk running across him. The restraining order had expired and he hadn't bothered her—yet.

The man groaned as he settled on his back.

Her lips parted. He was a mess. But he was a *hot* mess. Bits of grass mixed with rich brown strands. A neatly trimmed beard framed his chiseled face. Everything about him screamed strength and power. Quite a feat for an unconscious man. She didn't have to move his jacket and shirt around to know that he had a great body.

But she had no wish to touch his shirt. Blood was spattered across it. She couldn't see any open wounds. Not his blood? Her gaze swept his long body. No major injuries other than bloody knuckles.

Her jaw tightened. He was in a fight before he ended up here. Self-defense? Or was he a mean bastard? "What's your story?"

A smell hit her, and she wrinkled her nose. He smelled like a distillery. He'd either rolled in a vat of sanitizer, or a serious intake of alcohol caused his condition.

He shifted, like his mind was telling him to wake up but the alcohol was saying "No, baby, not yet."

That's when her gaze snagged on the waistband of his pants. His top and jacket were bunched so high that a lean line of skin was showing—over an open fly.

Was he pissing before he passed out? She pursed her lips. Fucking?

Why did she think that one was more likely? There was no one else around. And unless there was someone in another ditch, he was alone.

Passed out in the dried weeds, he was still gorgeous. Rugged, masculine, subtly threatening even while unconscious. So unlike men she usually dated.

Why was she standing over him, pondering her social life?

To be fair, it was *her* ditch he was passed out in and she had little social life. She could let him sleep it off, pretend she never saw him. Then she'd worry about him coming to and making his way to her house.

Better the enemy that she sort of knew than the one lurking around her place while she was trying to sleep.

She made up her mind. She handled Damian, she could handle…him.

She gently toed his belly. "Hey, buddy. Can you wake up?"

Maybe she should find a big stick in the trees behind her. Keep some distance between herself and him.

Another toe. "Dude. Wake up," she said louder.

He blinked an eye open, the startling clear brown capturing her in its gaze like a rabbit mesmerized by the beauty of the wolf about to eat it. "Hey, beautiful," he mumbled and passed out again.

Warmth cascaded over her. All because a strange man who looked and smelled like he had a night of debauchery called her beautiful.

Brushing it off, she stared down at him. Now what? He

seemed fine, but he couldn't lie out here and be a buffet for big, wild animals.

She stood up to angry, abusive men every week at her work. She'd managed to deal with one stalker.

She could deal with this man, too.

∼

SOMEONE'S TRYING to move me.

He grunted and tried to get out a "Lemme sleep" but the words garbled in his mouth.

Somewhere deep in his brain, his mind tried to sound an alarm. He was in a vulnerable position, surrounded by new scents.

But there was one scent he latched on to. Meadow flowers in full bloom. Just like home.

Home.

That was enough to rouse him, but the alcohol coursing through his system took him back under.

Memories bombarded him with each nudge to his gut. Flashes of a disappointed female. Him, jerking his dick out of her and stumbling away, unable to get either of them off and unwilling to try to any more. He'd been down that road for the last several months.

Her disappointment had turned to rage and more than a little misunderstanding with the patrons at the bar. Between her and the males jumping to her defense, assuming he'd done more than leaving her with a case of lady blue balls, he'd barely gotten out of the bar with a liter of whiskey and his limbs intact.

They'd pursued him.

More flashes traced through his brain. His maniacal laughter ringing in his ears as he dodged them during the search, a drunken game of hide-and-seek that took him farther into the surrounding woods until he was alone and stumbling along some road that went nowhere.

He groaned and rolled again. A voice cut through his hangover in the best way possible, washing over his eardrums like a cleansing waterfall.

"Hey. I can't carry you. If you want out of this ditch, you gotta get yourself to my car."

His drunken state was lasting longer, but only because he'd been out drinking later. Or earlier? The sun was coming up as he cleaned off the last drops. And he'd had a hell of a lot of hard liquor last night. But still, he was a shifter. He shouldn't have had a case of whiskey dick.

He faintly recalled opening his eyes and seeing an angel, halo and everything. But when he blinked open his dry eyes again...no, it was a woman with the sun behind her creating the halo effect. She was the source of the comforting smell that he wanted to get lost in.

He squinted at her. Her mouth moved, but he didn't care what she was saying, only what she looked like. Curvy. Petite for his kind.

Wait. He inhaled. She had a pleasing scent, but there was something that hadn't registered the first time. *Fuck*, she was human.

He passed out in the fucking woods and a human found him.

With a long moan, he rolled over and got to his hands and knees. The world spun and he almost crashed forward onto his head.

"Whoa, big guy. Not so fast."

He closed his eyes and leaned toward the musical chimes of her voice. The birds chirping were obnoxious as hell, but her...her voice was stirring things in him that he thought he'd lost. Namely, his libido.

But she was human.

He had a million problems, and messing with a human woman wasn't one.

"I got it," he grunted, but he doubted the words were intelligible.

"Oh, I can totally see that."

Her sarcasm made him pause. He squinted up at her again. "What's your name?" He had to know. He wouldn't move until he knew.

She planted her hands on nicely padded hips. The sun behind her still shadowed her face, but he was drinking his fill of her body. "Patience. And don't get it confused with a personality trait. I've been up all night and haven't had the chance to catch a few winks in my ditch like you, so if you don't mind, hustle your butt to my car."

Patience. He chuckled, the echo banging around in his head. No, it wasn't a personality trait. "Where are you taking me?"

Human hospitals were a no-no. He'd be sober in a few hours, hangover gone. He just needed to rest and not have to explain why his recovery was so much shorter. For one, it wasn't allowed.

He felt the retreat in her more than he could see it. She was reluctant and cautious. Smart girl.

"Um, my house is right up there. Since you're in a bad way and might lurch toward it when you come to, I thought we could just get it over with and I'd drive you the rest of the way. But if you're a psycho, just let me know. Save us both the headache."

He grinned again. With his face turned toward the ground, she couldn't see his longer and sharper canines. Blunt. He liked that. "Not a psycho, just a sad fuck who hasn't got his shit together."

"You don't say," she said dryly.

He laughed again. This wasn't what he expected to wake

up to, but maybe it was what he needed. His search for his sister—and doing it without his now happily mated twin brother—was taking him into darker mental territory than he was prepared to deal with.

Patience was both a wake-up call that he was risking the very laws he upheld, and a nice distraction.

"What about you?" he rasped, gazing up at her again. The sun had shifted, and he could make out a round face with full cheeks and quirked lips. Her gaze appraised him, and with his sharper vision, he could make out the light blue of her irises. "Are you a pervert waiting to take advantage of me?"

An eyebrow lifted. "I've been up all night, and I'm just crabby and want to sleep and not have my weekend of *Outlander* fucked up."

Outlander? Wasn't that a vehicle? "You can always leave me."

It'd be better for her, but he hoped she made the wrong choice. Because he didn't want to be done with impatient Patience yet.

Her cool appraisal came back, like she sensed his sincerity. She could leave him, and he'd be fine. A gusty sigh escaped her. "I've never left a stray alone."

He didn't have time to ponder what she meant before she was bending over him, helping him get to his feet.

He towered over her. There was at least a foot height difference between them, yet the security of her arm around his waist was strong.

"I feel obligated," she grunted as he swayed and she tried to stabilize him, "to inform you that your fly is open."

And with her so near, it was getting harder to not shame himself and send her running. He didn't want her to be rewarded for her Good Samaritan attempts by a raging erection waving in her face.

What happened to his flagging libido?

The grunt she let out pushing him up the incline of the ditch didn't help, either. He focused enough to fasten his pants. "Sorry. Hazard of a shitty night."

"I would think that smelling the way you do with your pants open meant it was a good night. But the blood on your shirt must be the shitty part?"

"No, that part was refreshing." Getting in a fight was a perfect way to release the desperate frustration building in him. He'd been on a solo mission for months and was no closer to finding any answers.

"You like to fight." Her disapproving tone made him want to hang his head in shame.

"No." His answer was honest as he lurched toward her silver sedan. He was the charmer who diffused situations and put people at ease. But he hadn't been himself lately. "Well, I don't usually. But last night, those guys just assumed the worst of me and attacked. So, I used it as an outlet."

"Huh." She didn't sound convinced.

What did he care?

Turned out, he cared more than he thought.

She left him to lean against her car as she opened the door and bent down to move the seat back all the way and clear off the surface of wrappers and a bag of something with a savory scent emanating from it.

The round, ripe ass facing him was one that he could sink his fangs into. Her leggings showed her underwear lines, and there was nothing fancy for her. Granny panties all the way.

Patience with the granny panties to his rescue.

He didn't realize he had a dopey grin until she turned and scowled at him. "Get in."

Right. She was cranky. "Yes, ma'am."

Were they plain white underwear? Or did she like the full coverage ones with cute prints?

His kind often passed on underwear. Just another article of clothing to discard when the time came to strip.

When she closed them in with her light blossom scent and drove to her house, he understood her comment about the rescues.

A three-legged dog limped, jumped, and whirled at the sight of her car. Cats scattered, but not far. They hung around the porch and the door of her little two-story cottage. There were at least three of them. One cat was missing an eye, and another had a permanent limp, but unlike the dog, he had all of his limbs. A red barn butted up against the trees with a penned-off portion on each side. One side had a couple of goats, and the other had chickens.

"You, uh, have a lot of animals."

"Yep."

Another dog came running to the car. A little heeler that was missing an ear. He stopped and cocked his head, his startling blue gaze on him.

Wishing he could talk to animals like one of his buddies, he assessed the dogs. Both were studying him now, and he tried to give off *I'm not harmless, but I won't harm her or you* vibes.

Most likely, they smelled the *I'm drunk as shit* vibe and did nothing more than thoroughly sniff him when he got out.

He didn't smell another man on her or in the surroundings. She was single. Just her and this menagerie.

"I can sleep in the barn," he said. Her place wasn't run down, but it was small and...well-loved. It was clear she wasn't rich, but did what she could to keep the place going. All these animals probably chewed through her earnings. He didn't need to burden her any more than he had.

"You could," she agreed. "But I saw the way you were eyeing my breakfast burrito, so why don't you come in, grab a bite after some real sleep. I know I need it."

He lurched around the car. The best thing to do would be to go sleep in a haystack and leave. She didn't know his name and he'd be nothing more than a weird occurrence in her blissfully normal human life.

But he was drawn to her house. Something inside him told him not to fight it, to just let it roll out. On-trend for how everything was going with her.

"Wait." She stopped him with her hands on his shoulders. He gazed down at her. She was even prettier than he initially thought. Without the ethereal appeal of the sun, he could see all her fine details. A few freckles sprinkled across her nose. Dusty brown brows that knit together as her gaze landed on the blood of his shirt. And a body that he could get lost in.

The females of his kind were often tall and lean, natural fighters like the males.

Patience was not a fighter.

Her pretty pink lips turned down and she reached up to ruffle his hair. Dried grass rained down.

"Just give you a little… Yep, don't want to drag that inside. I hate cleaning."

The corner of his mouth quirked up as blood swirled dizzily through his body, enough to make him grateful that he closed his fly. If she kept touching him, there'd be nothing he could do to keep his erection at bay. Add in the cute little stain on her shirt and she was all too approachable, but he wanted to do much more than approach her.

"I got it," he said too gruffly.

She snapped her hands back. "Sorry. Should've asked first. Don't forget your beard."

Abashed, he brushed at his face. Did he roll the last mile through the ditch before he passed out?

"You have nothing to be sorry for. Just show me where I can sleep this off and I'll be out of your hair."

Her hair. Were the light brown strands as soft as they

looked? He could sink his hands into it, pull her close and… probably get dumped back in that ditch.

"I'll get you settled and feed my beasts."

"I can help."

She eyed him dubiously. "Can you though?" Gentle sarcasm laced her words. Shaking her head, she quirked her lips. "Don't worry about it. I have a system and they expect it. You'll probably scare the goats and chickens."

She disappeared inside and he brushed himself off more, staggering as he did it, hoping he didn't repay her by stepping on one of her rescues' paws.

The dogs and cats had no self-preservation, sniffing around his boots. He was a predator. A supernatural predator. He could shift to a wolf and hunt them each down. But cats twined around his legs like he was a catnip-coated scratching post.

Patience opened the door, shooing away two cats that tried to dart outside. "The couch is ready."

He stumbled into her place, shrugging out of his coat. She took it from him and hung it on a hook, safely away from the rest of her coats. Good thing, too. He still stunk like that bar, not like the warm, inviting scent of her home.

The place smelled like her, but homier. Comforting. Welcoming. It was a small house with a distinct seventies flair that hadn't been updated. It was well-kept like the yard, the fading yellow flowered wallpaper was in good condition and the hardwood floor polished to a shine—with a healthy sprinkling of fur.

The two cats had retreated to the back of the couch and were staring at him. One looked so old he could rival the elders of Malcolm's kind. And the other was missing an eye. What were their Patience rescue stories?

He wanted to know too damn much about the human. He needed sleep so he could handle himself around her. Pulling off his shirt, he stopped when Patience made a choking noise.

Did he scare her? "I'm not stripping. I just don't want to get blood on your furniture."

"Yeah, that's what I'm worried about." Her eyes stroked over his chest while she furiously blushed.

Was she scared for her safety? He tried to play it cool. "I don't suppose you have a pair of boxers I could borrow?"

Her mouth worked and her forehead crinkled but her gaze didn't leave his pecs. "My brother might have left... No, actually, it wouldn't fit anyway. Don't worry about it. I laid down a sheet."

Pressure from the last several months and the dogged failure of his personal mission sloughed off him. For the first time in a long time, he was at ease. His wolf was at ease. He could rest here.

"Thank you," he said hoarsely, unable to communicate how much this meant to him.

She canted her head to peer up at him. "What's your name, stranger?"

He should stick with 'stranger,' but he said, "Malcolm."

"Nice to meet you, Malcolm. Don't piss on the couch in your sleep."

CHAPTER 2

*H*e was so big.

Patience hovered at the bottom of the stairs. They ended at the edge of her living room and she had a clear shot of the big man she rescued slumbering on her couch. He was on his back, the patterned quilt she gave him was tucked up to his chest and he had one arm bent behind his head, his biceps flexing in that mouthwatering way she hardly ever got to see in real life.

But how was he doing?

The living room had a faint whiff of alcohol. He'd been sleeping it off for a while.

Hazard of a shitty night.

She usually dealt with the other gender, but she could tell when a person was running from their problems. Malcolm might not be running exactly, but he wasn't dealing well with whatever was eating at him.

What was going on in his world? What was his world even like?

She wanted to know so much about him, but she suppressed a wistful sigh. As if a guy like him would ever

17

look twice at a girl like her. Muscled, hot man with hints of a witty sense of humor falls for frumpy loner who rescues strays, and her cats like him, too.

Traitors. They usually scattered when people like her neighbor's sister-in-law came to taunt her. The neighbors, she liked. The sister-in-law, not so much. She held a grudge against Patience that she never understood. But her neighbors never witnessed the encounters, so Patience assumed they remained oblivious. To think otherwise would be depressing as fuck, and it was nothing she couldn't handle.

"You can take a picture," his deep voice rumbled, breaking into her thoughts. "It'll last longer."

She jumped and let out a squeak. Chip and Dale, her two indoor cats, barely registered her startle. They were curled up between his side and the back of the couch, making it look like Malcolm sprouted mold growths overnight. Chip cracked an eyelid and looked disapprovingly at her for waking his heating pad, and shut it again.

She'd been so careful not to make a sound coming down the stairs.

"I didn't want to wake you," she said primly because she was *not* staring. She clutched her fluffy pink robe tighter at the neck and strode to the back of the couch to peer imposingly down at him. Gah. He looked even hotter with a sleepy grin and cats littered over him. "I figured you'd be resting longer after the beating you took. It'll take more than a nap to heal after what you went through."

Something flickered in his eyes that she couldn't identify. "Right. I'm pretty, uh, sore and stuff."

He sounded like he was trying to convince her. Was he afraid she'd kick him out as soon as he was better?

Was she afraid she wouldn't?

"I'm going to make breakfast for supper. Is your appetite back?"

He appraised her with intense brown eyes. "My appetite never left."

It had to be the robe she threw on over her holey Minnesota Twins T-shirt and bunny print flannel pajama pants that swamped her with heat. Because not even a hot guy was reason enough to get her to dress up at home. She didn't lack for confidence, but she was realistic about her type. And drunk-in-a-ditch-handsome was still out of her league.

"Okay. I'll make some eggs and sausage."

He frowned slightly. "Don't you want me to leave?"

Her mouth tipped up at the corner. "I usually rehab strays before deciding whether I can release them into the wild. You haven't even sat up yet. Seems too early to make the decision."

What was she doing? Dragging a strange man home and coddling him? Were her last few dates really that bad? Well, yes. But was she that desperate? She could write off bad dates, but this was a little harder to explain.

Yet, despite his size and how little she knew about him, her instinct said he wasn't any danger to her or her animals.

"I'll take the stray comment, but it's not your job to rehab me." His words weighed heavier. He wasn't saying it lightly.

Loneliness rolled off him. A sense of being rudderless. Was she attuned to his feelings because she worked with people like him—lost and alone even when surrounded by others—or because it's how she felt?

"Just being a decent person. As long as you don't rape and murder me, I really don't mind. Unless *Outlander* quits streaming and I miss the last few seasons. Then I'll never forgive you."

His lips twitched. "What the hell is *Outlander*?"

She'd watch it with him, start at the beginning even, but there were enough sex scenes to make it unbearable for her to sit through with him—and highly awkward for Malcolm. He might think she was trying to seduce him.

She wasn't a seducer, as her exes liked to point out. More than one had said *You'd rather hang out with your animals than go out with me.*

You haven't given me a reason yet to want to spend more time with you.

But back to *Outlander*. "It's a show. And a book. A show from a book." She cleared her throat. The way he was eyeing her made her wonder if her fluffy pink robe was see-through. "I'll go cook."

He sat up, careful not to dislodge Chip and Dale. They blinked and stretched and hopped over the back of the couch and meandered to the kitchen. Malcolm's stomach rippled, staying all washboard as shit, as he sat.

It wasn't fair.

He ran a hand through his hair and grimaced. "Mind if I shower first? I'd offer to help cook, but you don't want me around edible stuff when I'm like this."

She blinked, her gaze raking his body, but not solely out of interest. Not one bruise. If he was the winner of the fight, wouldn't he still be bruised?

And he didn't talk like he had a raging headache. That wasn't an *oops, it spilled on me* level of booze. The way he smelled, he'd had a lot to drink. How could he not be hungover? And he woke when she came downstairs without making one stair creak.

Add in that he was devastating to look at, to want to be around. Tall, dark, and handsome.

All the pieces clicked into place. Given where she lived, who her neighbors were, she shouldn't be surprised. He was a shifter. Now, she just had to pretend she didn't know what he was. Fly under the radar of his kind. Only those she helped knew that she and her brother knew about them and they wouldn't report them.

Patience and Jacob helped all species, and that included people like Malcolm. Only, his kind's leaders wouldn't take so kindly to what they'd done and what they continued to do.

His eyes had narrowed while she pondered him. What had he asked? Oh, yes. "The bathroom is upstairs." And thankfully, clean for once. She'd dumped her underclothes in the dirty laundry so nothing embarrassing should be lying around. "You can, like, tie a sheet toga-style around yourself and I'll throw your clothes in the wash."

"No need for you to do that. Point me toward the laundry room and a clean sheet."

She gestured to the other side of the stairs and scurried into the kitchen.

She had a shifter male. In her house. Of course she'd bring someone like him home. A spinster with a farmyard of rescues finds the man of her dreams and he's not a man.

She tucked her hair behind her ears, thinking for the first time that she should've done something with it. She had two hairstyles—down and ponytail. Just like she had two clothing looks. Presentable enough for work, and bad enough for chores.

Whipping eggs, she focused on her task and not her looks. She needed to kick her insecurity to the curb. She was helping him. She wasn't looking for more and neither was he.

The shower kicked off upstairs, rattling the pipes in the walls. The sausage was almost done and since she was a responsible adult, she fried some potatoes and onions. It was well-rounded enough, in a greasy sort of way. Since her guest probably had more of an appetite than the average guy, she doubled her initial amounts.

"Smells good."

She glanced over her shoulder and nearly swallowed her tongue. Wide shoulders poked out of his toga sheet and strong legs stuck out the bottom. He could start a new fashion trend. His drying hair was slicked off his face, showing the hard angle of his nose and his carved cheekbones. Not even his beard could hide the cut of his chin.

The beard thing... She never thought she'd be into it, but yeah. She was into it. "We can eat and then when your clothes are dry, I can give you a ride to town."

Did she imagine the flash of disappointment in his eyes? "My truck is still probably at the bar."

"Which bar?"

"Razor's Edge." His tone was cautious and heat swept through her body as he focused on her, waiting for a response.

She nodded, acting like it was just another bar she drove past every day in her tiny town of Twin Forks. That was a bit of a misnomer—Twin Forks comprised a scattering of nearby small towns with all the amenities in Twin Forks proper. Why Razor's Edge settled in Twin Forks was a mystery, but it wasn't a normal bar. People like her would run screaming from the rough and sexually charged crowd of Razor's Edge.

Where shifters got together and satisfied their baser instincts.

They're horny assholes, her brother had said when he told her about it shortly after she was of legal age to drink and wanted to go there. *You'll find a place like that in communities with a high number of shifters. They have some name that'll give you a clue, like the one called Pale Moonlight in West Creek. A hub of fornication, but I guess it's a way to find mates outside of their packs.*

Malcolm shuffled over to a cupboard and opened it. Oh,

shit. How would she explain what was in there? Grandma had kept a boatload of salt on hand and Patience had never moved it. There was enough to do around the house.

"Not that one," she said quickly.

He closed it and moved to the next one. A grunt of approval came out of that broad chest as he grabbed two plates. She relaxed. He did the same with the drawers, looking for silverware, while she flipped potatoes, getting them as crispy as they could be without being burned.

She didn't know what drove her to say what she was thinking, teasing him, but it came out anyway. "I was going to use paper plates, but I guess I'll do dishes too…" She snorted out a laugh as his eyes flared. "Just kidding. I probably don't have any."

He chuckled and shook his head. "So getting a couple of glasses is safe?"

"Sure. There's OJ and milk and water. I don't have anything stronger."

"I don't think I need anything stronger for a while."

"I dunno. There's a lot of ditches around Razor's Edge, but I can't promise the ambiance of your next rescuer's place will be any better than this." She waved the spatula around her old, faded kitchen. It was tidy, but like the rest of the house, worn and sun-bleached because she liked to open the blinds and windows as much as her grandma did.

He shook his head, a rueful expression on his face. "Funny, but I'm not leaving your ditch any more than a three-star review."

"Harsh. Was it the toe to the gut to wake you?"

"No, it was the burs poking me in the ass."

She laughed, the sound ringing off the walls. Her *Outlander* marathon was the highlight of her weekends, but once she returned Malcolm to wherever he came from, it was going to seem like a consolation prize.

~

MALCOLM FOUGHT THE GUILT OFF. He ate every scrap of food she made and didn't eat herself.

Savory sausage that wasn't cheap shit thrown together from lips and assholes and sold at rock bottom price. Potatoes he suspected came from her own garden or someone else's because you can't buy that level of creaminess in store-bought spuds. And eggs that damn near made him orgasm—which had been impossible enough lately.

If his kind didn't have to deal with fated mates and all that bullshit, he'd say she got to his heart through his stomach. But no one could get to his heart because his mate ripped it out, stomped on it, and mated someone else.

"Are you sure you don't want more?" He was a bastard, eyeing the food on her plate as she finished up. He was full, but he'd eat more on principle. Who knew when he'd get that kind of home-cooked meal again?

His work kept him busy and not in one place for long enough. That was the excuse he used. Usually he risked the heartburn, got bar food, and fucked all night.

"I'm fine. I have chores yet and don't like to do those on a super full stomach. Besides." She pushed around her potatoes, strategically loading them onto her fork. She probably used her fingers when she was alone, and he wished he could assure her that she could do that now. But then he'd want to lick them off. "I'll probably wind up grabbing a few groceries with a healthy amount of junk food before I come back home."

Right. She was taking him back to town. To get the beat-up pickup he used to share with his brother. It was all his now. Because he was all by himself and his twin had someone to go home to every night.

His chest ached. He'd take that over sporting a hard-on

through this thin sheet. Even if she was interested—and he could smell that she was trying not to be—he couldn't treat her like she didn't mean anything.

She was special. Just not for him.

He rose. "My clothes are probably ready for the dryer. Don't do dishes. I'll do them after the laundry."

"Deal. The critters are hungry and it's almost their normal feeding time."

Questions he'd pondered before but had other things to worry about, like not falling on top of her and accidentally assaulting her with the surprise erection she'd given him, came to mind. "Do you work nights?"

"Not usually." Her moves became clipped. She didn't want to talk about her work. She acted the same when it came to Razor's Edge, but then that place might have a nasty reputation among humans. The humans who did frequent the place weren't soft and humorous like Patience. "It was a surprise triple shift. I'll have to get my hours back to normal over the weekend."

When was the last time he lounged around for a weekend? Last year, he and Harrison were the bodyguards for Harrison's now-mate, Sylva. It was like this. Calm. Pleasant. Almost like he had his own place in the world with people who wanted him. But it was still a mission, doing nothing but hinting at what he'd never have.

Harrison might've found the will to mate after what happened to his fated mate, but she hadn't left him willingly. Malcolm's had. Willingly and ruthlessly.

He formulated a response for when she asked about what he was doing in Twin Forks and what he did for work, but she never asked.

As he promised, he did his own laundry and then washed and dried the dishes. The house was small and intuitive. He made his way around without having to pepper Patience with questions. Which was good, because she wasn't around. By the time he was done with laundry, she'd gone outside.

He finished the dishes and put the plates in the right cupboard. Not the spice cupboard he'd opened earlier. The one with no less than five containers of off-brand salt. He'd expected the eggs to be a salty overload if she loved it that much, but they were perfect. Not even his kind kept that much salt.

He wandered outside. She might need help.

Was that an excuse to be around her? Of course, she didn't need help. She lived out here alone. He scented only her and the animals. Not the brother she mentioned and not any males she held onto long enough for their scent to permeate.

When he spotted her, he had to stop, a smile playing over his lips. She clucked through the chicken pen in bright yellow rain boots, murmuring and making noises that the chickens seemed to respond to, only because she was doling out their feed and refreshing their water.

The nip in the air pinked her cheeks and the stocking hat on her head hid her beautiful mane of hair but gave her a snow bunny appeal.

As he stood, cats twined around his legs. How the hell was he going to help her in a sheet?

"Stupid." After stooping to give each of the three cats a scratch behind the ears, he went inside to check the dryer.

His clothes were mostly done, with just a hint of dampness. He put them on and went back to the door. He stepped into his boots and inspected his black leather jacket. It reeked of sex, blood, and booze. He couldn't bring himself to put it on and stifle Patience's lovely scent.

It wasn't that cold outside, not for him anyway. Patience's delectable body was hidden by a worn and baggy sweater. He stepped back out just as she filled the cat and dog dishes on the porch.

"All ready, I see?" Breath puffed out of her mouth.

His gaze was riveted to her lips when he felt the telltale pressure around his legs. The cats had bypassed their food to rub up on him.

"I'm surprised they're so comfortable around you." She pressed her lips together and he sensed her regret at what she'd said.

"Me, too," was all he could reply. The three-legged dog flopped at his feet and rolled to show his belly. He clearly thought Malcolm was dominant. He was right.

Her mouth pursed. "That's my guard dog, Tripod."

"I'd ask how he got the name—"

"I was going to call him Threefer." She grinned, her blue eyes dancing. "He got caught in a trap. That's how he lost his leg. Then he got nicked by a car. Then he tangled with a—a… wolf." Her gaze darted away.

"I'm surprised he survived the last two."

"The wolf one was scary. I got there in time. Me and my shotgun. The other dog is Shaggy."

He scanned the trees crowding in on her property. With all her animals, coyotes and wolves probably thought her place was an easy target. Tripod and the other dog were better than nothing.

"I'll change shoes and we can head to town." She breezed past him and the sense of dismissal she left him with soured his mood.

He didn't want to leave. He could picture himself plopping down on the porch and letting the cats roam over him, petting the dogs, and enjoying the vivid sunset through the trees.

He let out a long breath, gave her place one last look, and

went to wait by her car. He roamed around the car, kicking lightly at the tires.

When Patience appeared in athletic shoes, wearing the same of everything else, he couldn't look at her. She was everything he couldn't have, and he was everything she wanted to get rid of. She had a kind heart, but other than that, he was nothing more than a rescue. Physical attraction was one thing, but she was a smart woman and seemed to sense he was bad news for her.

"I'm surprised you have a car with all those gravel roads," he said mostly to distract himself from the melancholy line of thinking.

She shrugged as she got in, not having bothered to lock her doors this far out of town. "Every time I save up some money, I find another stray." She nodded toward the goats. "A woman in town raised them to make soap with and she had to go into a home. No one would take them, so I asked her to teach me her ways and they're mine now. Only one gives milk anymore."

He thought back to the plain slivers of pleasing soap in her shower. They didn't overpower his senses, which was easy to do with commercial products. "You make your own soap?"

She nodded as she climbed in. "My work... I give what I don't use away. It's cheaper and not full of the fake perfumes that are hard on...some people. You know, people with allergies and stuff."

Her movements got jerky again. She really didn't like talking about her job.

She started down the road. Neither of them said anything when they passed the spot she found him in. He half expected a smart-assed comment, since that seemed to be her thing. But a tiny lined formed in her brow. She was deep in thought.

He could be too, but then he'd think about her. This woman with a load of salt who saved dogs from wolves and—

Her reaction when she relayed the story came back to him. What was it about the wolves? And the salt?

That was a lot of salt. He knew what his kind needed salt for. Silver poisoning. What else did humans use it for?

Did she preserve her own food? She'd gotten jumpy when he looked in the cupboard.

Wolves. Salt. No questions about how fast he healed and his lack of a hangover.

I'm surprised they're so comfortable around you.

She reacted oddly after she'd said that, too. And she didn't say it about her dog that submitted itself. Shouldn't her dog also be wary of someone like him?

He studied her. Her eyes flicked nervously around. Her scent bloomed in the cab and he'd been trying to ignore it lest his blood rush to his dick again like it tended to do around her.

He smelled a faint thread of deceit buried in her meadow blossom scent.

What did Patience know?

She was a recluse. He knew from his work that those type of people usually saw more than the typical person. They paid attention.

What did Patience pay attention to?

As a Guardian, the police force of his people, he kept tabs on humans who knew of shifters and weren't mates. Humans who weren't mates weren't supposed to know about shifters. Often, Guardians had to wipe humans' minds of their interactions.

He was a fuck-up in a lot of ways, but he was damn good at his job. And his gut told him that this little human with her lack of questions and her abundance of salt knew exactly what he was.

They were coming to a curve and beyond that was a straight stretch. Time to temporarily put aside his personal mission and do his job. "Stop the car, Patience."

CHAPTER 3

*T*he way he said it sent shivers tumbling down her spine. His voice was low, serious. He'd been polite and irreverent, but the Malcolm in the car with her right now was grim and intense.

Her body sparked alive.

No. *No*. She didn't do dominance.

Stopping the car with him in the middle of nowhere seemed like a bad idea. "Why?"

"So you can tell me how you know what I am."

A tremble replaced the shiver. *Shit*. What had she done to give herself away? It's not like she brandished her shotgun with silver pellets.

The salt cupboard?

She pulled to a stop, pulling over as far as possible even though no other motorists would be on this road unless they were lost.

He twisted in a seat that was too small for him and faced her, his expression carved from rock.

The stories she heard about how diligently shifters

policed their own kind were nothing but tales until this point. What did Malcolm do for his world? He acted like more than a concerned shifter citizen.

She fiddled her fingers together and avoided his gaze. How should she approach this? An *I don't know what you're talking about, I'm just a lonely, eccentric woman*?

Or was it better to lie by telling only parts of the truth?

Since the level of intelligence in his eyes had only increased the longer he'd been awake, that might be the best approach.

"Look at where I live," she finally said. "A lot of weird stuff happens and people talk—"

"What people." He didn't ask it as a question. He demanded.

Her belly fluttered. *Bad timing and a bad choice, Patience.* She could not get hung up on a male like him.

"Old people." He wouldn't mess with the elderly, would he? "Look, I've just seen enough over the years to pair it all together with the old wives' tales."

He stared at her, the corners of his jaw flexing. "Turn around and drive back to your place."

Just a few minutes ago, she was sad to see him go. Now she didn't want him near her. The stories she heard were from shifters themselves. Malcolm was a stranger. He might be one of the ones they were running from.

"Why?" Her voice trembled.

"Because the smell of your fear is going to choke me. You might as well be in your space when we talk."

"I'm not scared," she snapped. And she wasn't, not of him, she realized. She was anxious about what he might do, who he might report her to, and what they might find out. That unknown she was terrified of.

"Then you're hiding something." He folded his arms. "So we'll talk here. How do you know about the salt?"

"If I knew about the salt, I'd also know that it helps save your sorry ass if you get silver in you. I'd have it to help." Because some of the shifters she'd helped over the years had needed it.

"Want me to search your house? I bet I'll find something silver that's more than a pretty pair of earrings."

Her eyes widened and it didn't escape his notice. It was one thing to have shifters come to her for help, and another to be faced with an irritated one. "You aren't searching my house. You can't."

She'd heard of the team of shifters that police their kind, but she doubted one of them would've been drunk in her ditch. Besides, if he was one, wouldn't he need a warrant or something?

He couldn't be one. Her luck with men—or males— wouldn't be that shitty.

"I can and I will."

She shot him a cool look. "What if I call the police?"

"You won't even remember my name."

Another threat. She'd been told they could make her forget. "And what gives you the right?"

"I'm tasked by my people as a Guardian to protect them."

Her stomach plummeted. Hello, shitty fortune. But then if she'd been graced with an easy life, she wouldn't still be living in her grandma's old house with hardly any memories of her parents.

"We have our own laws," he continued. "And since you know of us, you must now abide by them."

She sighed and stared out the windshield for a moment, kicking her car in gear, but she didn't turn around. "I should've left you in that ditch. You could've walked back to town."

"Turn around, Patience."

She flicked her gaze in his direction and arched a brow.

"Didn't you say you have a pickup at Razor's Edge where you were fornicating and getting plastered?" He winced. Her description was uncomfortably accurate. She almost grinned. "So I'm assuming that it'd be best if you had said truck. You can drive it back to my place and finish your interrogation."

Had she just invited him back to her place? He had threatened to search it, but she didn't want him going through her belongings. All he'd find incriminating was the silver shot she rarely needed for her shotgun. They kept the bulk of it at the center. That was about all she was hiding—at her house anyway.

In her head, she had a lot of information that'd get her and Jacob in deep trouble with Malcolm's people.

"Or, you can talk on the way to town," he said.

Her luck sucked. He'd wipe her mind and forget about her at best. "Tell me why no human but a mate can know about shifters."

"Torture, death, exposure. Do you think we'd be allowed to live peacefully?" He huffed. "We'd be tagged, tracked, and studied on a good day."

She'd go with the "not all humans" argument, but it'd take only a few to make trouble. From what she knew, their populations weren't large and they were very isolated. Except for Freemont, which was south of Twin Forks, but the main pack of Guardians was across the river from Freemont in West Creek.

Time for some of that truth. "My brother and I had been living with our grandmother for a few years—that's the same place I live in now—when we were outside doing chores. Our chickens had been hit again, but unlike a fox or coyotes, whatever hit the chickens didn't leave a bloody mess behind. The chickens were—poof!— gone. So, being the ambitious kids who'd heard stories their whole life that we were, went searching for them. Grandma needed that egg money to raise us."

Patience navigated the roads, lost in the past, and hoping he bought her story. She didn't have to tell him *how* she and Jacob knew what to search for. "We searched the woods for two days before we found her. Beaten, terrified, and half-wild." Not shifter feral. If she'd been feral, and someone like Malcolm found her, she might've been put down. The female said she was rogue and Patience learned over and over again what that meant for their kind. "She didn't sense us before she tried to shift, but she couldn't complete a full transition."

"That had to be scary for a couple of kids." The compassion in his tone gave her hope that he'd consider her situation before he did anything drastic.

"It was. But when she settled back in her human form, she wept. We helped her and she told us what to do. She was weak from silver poisoning. I guess she'd been stealing from the neighbors, who were old like Grandma at the time, and had taken all the salt she could. But Grandma kept a shotgun and another injury would've done her in."

"Then what?"

They were in town now. Her tidy little unexciting town—to everyone but her and Jacob. She and her brother, who knew what else lived among them. They helped those who wanted to get away, and they also knew what that could cost them.

"I don't know. We gave her some salt. She told Grandma how to get the silver out, and by morning she was gone."

That part was all true.

His mouth was set in a firm line. He was probably thinking about how he might have to find out who it was and where she went. Supposedly a shifter without a pack, and especially without a mate, started having issues with reality. Slowly went insane. Risked exposure of what they were.

But the ones that she and Jacob had helped over the years sometimes just needed out of their own packs. Needed the freedom to choose.

Shifters like her stepmother.

HE INHALED DEEPLY, trying to sort through her scents. They were all the same as before, but he smelled her resolve. He smelled all of her. He hated that she acted anxious around him now, and not like the snarky woman who hauled his ass out of the weeds. He hated that she didn't want to look at him and that overall, he scared her. Maybe not him personally, but what he could order done to her.

She shouldn't know about them. The shifter she and her brother helped all those years ago should've been tracked down and returned to her pack, or at least ensured that she joined another.

Not all packs let their members leave. Was that the case?

How many years ago was it? Patience looked to be around thirty, maybe a little older. Two kids naive enough to be searching the woods for a chicken-stealing shifter would've been how old? Twelve? Fourteen?

He didn't know kids. He really didn't know human kids. Regardless, what she described had to have occurred fifteen or more years ago. If the female had gone feral, she'd have made enough trouble to be found by now.

"Did the female give her name?" He could report any details back to his boss, Commander Fitzsimmons.

"No."

He breathed in deep, steeling himself against all things meadow blossoms. She was telling the truth. Still, something about her story didn't sit straight with him.

Patience was savvy. She lived on her own and had passed under the Guardian's radar for at least fifteen years. The story she told him might be true, but she might be leaving a metric ton out.

He suspected the latter.

Drumming his fingers on his knee, he contemplated this situation while she drove. He was looking for his sister. He'd taken a sabbatical from his work, and he'd been allowed to because his commander rightfully suspected that his head wasn't on straight after Harrison's mating.

He could afford to linger in Twin Forks a little longer. The boss would understand once he was briefed.

The idea of telling Commander Fitzsimmons about Patience made his fangs throb. He didn't want another shifter around her.

So that meant he'd be hanging around for a while. Using some of his time to figure out her story. "Is your grandma still alive?"

Her hand tightened on the wheel. "She passed away years ago."

"And your brother?"

Her mouth tightened. "He lives in town." She eyed him, fear hidden in the depths of her eyes. "Are you going to talk to him?"

"Not if you tell me what I need to know."

"How do I know you are who you say you are?"

It was a smart question. It's not like they were badge-carrying beings. They said they were Guardians and shifters can smell a lie. Patience would just have to believe him. "You don't, but you can trust me."

She rolled her eyes toward him, then back to stare out the windshield.

"You can, Patience. I don't need to lie to do my job."

"Okay. Then what are you doing in Twin Forks? And why were you drunk and in the middle of nowhere?"

Damn, she went right for it. "That wasn't part of my job."

"So, your personal life is a mess?"

He lifted a shoulder, not caring if she saw him shrug or not. "Regardless, it's not a part of my work."

"So you were off duty and now you're on duty?"

An explanation fought to spill out. He could tell her how Guardians worked, but how he and his twin were different because their father was once a Lycan Council member, but when the council became too corrupt, he and Harrison helped overthrow it. But they were often farmed out to be part of the Guardian pack that worked for their new government, the Synod. He and Harrison were a link to the past but enforced the future. It made the transition easier. And he got to visit his father, who was happily sitting in jail, versus going back to his hometown to face his mate.

He could tell her how Harrison found his mate and how that left Malcolm alone now. They used to work together, fight together, fuck females together. But his twin had become a happy fucker and Malcolm was pathetically lost.

He wanted to go on and tell her about his sister and how she disappeared and how it ate at him that he could never find her. And that finding her now was the only thing keeping him from drowning himself in the bottom of a bottle.

But he didn't. Because he was a Guardian and he couldn't trust her.

"I was on vacation," was all he said. "And once I figured out that you knew what I was, I went back on duty."

"What a Boy Scout," she muttered.

He chuckled. What had he expected from a woman who dragged his sorry ass home to sleep it off? "We might as well get to know each other. What's your last name?"

"Why? Are you going to call your people and do some in-depth search?"

"What would I find?"

"That Patience Montgomery is one boring woman. She's never been arrested, she's never gotten a ticket, and the only time she's been in an accident was when Old Man Woodward backed his tractor into her front bumper."

"At your place?"

"No. At the grocery store. He thought getting his license suspended didn't extend to taking farm equipment to get his Lucky Charms."

He fought a smile. Patience was the least-boring person he'd ever met.

Razor's Edge appeared and he pointed to his lone old truck. "That one's mine."

"Left your black SUV with tinted windows home for the weekend?" If she wasn't asking so sarcastically, he would've been alarmed she knew so many details about Guardians.

"My brother and I used to share, but he's newly mated." He bit the inside of his lip. What was he doing telling her that stuff?

She maneuvered next to his vehicle, parking on the driver's side. "You guys were, like, partners?"

"He's my twin," he said, as if that were enough explanation.

"So he's at his home. I didn't miss him on the other side of the road?"

She was only teasing, but it reminded him how alone he was. "No."

She shrugged, but her expression was kind. "Is your twin being newly mated one of the personal reasons that made you drain the bottle last night?"

It concerned him how badly he wanted to answer her, so he only scowled. "Meet you at home, Patience."

Once he got out, he realized how familiar what he said sounded. *Home.* After Harrison mated, they gave up their bachelor pad near Synod headquarters. Malcolm didn't have a home. He had a job and he risked fucking that up.

Patience rolled down the window but continued to back out. "Since you know the way, I won't wait for you."

Her laughter trailed after the vehicle.

Fuck. He hadn't paid attention on the way into town, and last night who knew how the hell he ended up that far out of town? He hadn't even shifted when he took off running. He'd just stumbled along roads, muttering to himself and draining his second liter.

Yet, when he hopped behind the wheel, he couldn't stop the twist to his lips. She was ballsy. He fired up the engine but stayed close to the speed limit, trying not to lose her. Since she obviously knew the way well, it was harder with each block.

He was easing away from an empty four-way stop when movement caught his eye. A woman was walking a couple of blocks away. He glanced over and blinked. A familiar shade of hair and a swaying backside blazed into his mind.

Impossible.

There was no way the mate who left him for someone else would be in Twin Forks.

Was he so stuck in the past that he was starting to hallucinate? Why her? He should be catching glimpses, real or not, of his sister, Camille.

He'd swing around to check it out, but Patience was getting farther away and he wasn't sure he could get back on his own without hanging his head out the window and sniffing his way like a hound dog.

A quiet observation echoed loud in his mind. He was bypassing a possible sighting of his fated mate for a snarky human woman who was lying to him.

But his fated mate chose someone else. So if that was her, it'd only bring him more heartache to see her again. And following Patience was part of his duty, the job he'd sworn his life to.

And without his job, he was nothing.

CHAPTER 4

*P*atience went inside when she arrived home and put her rain boots on. On the way home, she'd had time for a hurried call to Jacob. He was going to notify their father to stay far away from Twin Forks and especially from her place. The odds that their dad would come back home after being gone since she was a kid were slim, but it was better to be safe in this case.

As for the other shifters she'd helped, she hoped they knew the drill to treat her like an oblivious human if they crossed paths again.

By the time she banged back out the door, Malcolm was pulling up. He parked beside her car in the little loop that curved by her barn and around to the house. His stormy expression made her belly clench and she had to look away.

The old garage was situated next to the house, but she would never fit her car inside. It contained all of her grandma's many collections and projects. She couldn't bring herself to get rid of them yet. The few times she'd tried, she ended up depressed, missing the grandma who filled the role of the mother and father Patience never really knew.

Her grandma was all she had growing up. Her older brother Jacob dedicated his life to his work and was also single. They were the last of their line. Two lonely kids who became lonely adults.

What would happen to the house when she was gone?

Her heart caught in her throat and she blinked away the burn in her eyes before Malcolm got out of his pickup. Each year that passed only amplified her feelings. It had nothing to do with waking up to a guy in her house and wondering what life could've been like had Twin Forks been bigger, with more options. Her work was rewarding and all, and she loved her animals, but she'd grown up assuming that she'd have a family.

Her furry family was enough. It had to be.

The click of the vehicle door ripped her out of her head. Malcolm's dark gaze landed on her. Was she fooling herself that there was a spark of concern in his eyes? Did he sense her feelings?

It didn't matter. She went from being his rescuer to nothing more than a job, and she had to make sure he thought nothing was wrong here, other than her knowledge of his kind.

"Chores?" he asked as he swaggered closer, his gaze dropping to her yellow rain boots.

"I have to clean the chicken pen." She shot him a smug grin. "Want to help?"

"Sure." His answering smile was even cockier.

Drat. He wasn't scared off by feathers and chicken poop. He'd probably seen a lot in his day. Which prompted another question. "How old are you, anyway?"

He crossed his arms, his biceps flexing in his muscle shirt. "Older than you."

Right. This was a get to know *her* situation, not a get to know each other weekend. She was nothing more than a job.

"But not by more than a couple decades," he finally answered, sending tingles of warmth through her belly. "If that."

She was thirty, so he was middle-aged in human years. Just a young shifter, from what she understood of their lifespans. "You sure you want to get shit on your boots?"

"I have another pair."

She glanced at his pickup. He was now stocked with changes of clothes. She'd have to mourn the toga-wearing guy in her kitchen later.

"All right."

He did whatever she told him to. They cleaned the chicken coop and then the goats were next. Her cats and dogs followed Malcolm around like they decided to form a pack and assigned him as the leader.

Ironic.

As long as she had help, and since the last thing she wanted to do was hang out in her tiny living room with a guy she just met—who might punish her, and not in a fun bedroom way—she put Malcolm to work changing out the cat and dog bedding and freshening up their area of the barn.

Then they swept the porch, cleaned her garden beds, and hauled the goat manure to her flower beds. With each new task she thought of, Malcolm leveled his steady gaze on her.

Before she shooed him away to haul another load of manure to the garden, she said, "You're free to leave at any time."

He only shook his head and pushed the wheelbarrow away, giving her a chance to sneak into the barn and peek at her phone. A text from Jacob that said he'd gotten ahold of their father.

Disappointment snaked through her. Dad didn't text her himself, but he was probably being overly cautious. Jacob assumed the risk of knowing Dad's phone number and messaging him.

She missed Dad. For all intents and purposes, she and Jacob were supposed to pretend he was dead. For the rest of their lives.

Returning her phone to her sweater pocket, she went to check on her free labor. Though, looking at his big body slinging and spreading black gold over the soil, it dawned on her that just because he didn't charge, didn't mean he was free.

She'd have to feed him. Good thing she hated grocery shopping and stocked her pantry and freezers. But Malcolm's appetite wouldn't be like an older brother's occasional visit.

That body burned fuel as easily as it burned her senses. And he claimed he was staying with her. Three meals a day. Together.

She watched him, mesmerized.

He dressed in all black, but his muscles rippled under his shirt and through the denim of his black pants. He'd left his jacket in the pickup, and while she could tolerate the cool weather with a sweater because she was moving around, he didn't appear affected.

Tossing the rake in the wheelbarrow with the shovel, he clapped his hands. Dust flung around him, glinting in the sun and causing a halo effect around him.

She'd really never seen a male as fine as him. Shifters were usually tall and she'd never seen one without an impressive physique. The ones she'd met never packed on extra pounds from a sweet tooth they indulged too regularly.

But Malcolm was next-level. She had to quit noticing and evaluating. Just being around him ruined her for other men.

He tossed his shovel in the wheelbarrow and she didn't hide her scrutiny as he zoomed by her. She followed him into the barn. What else could she have him do? This wasn't a big place, but it required a lot of care. TV binge or not, she wouldn't have gotten all this done this weekend and she would've needed ibuprofen each night for some mystery ache.

She scanned the neat inside of the barn, trying to find something he could clean. Her gaze tracked over the goat pens and the shelving that could use an upgrade. Maybe he was good with a hammer—

A wall of heat smacked into her. Her breath caught in her throat and she backed up. He towered over her. She stumbled back, but he caught her arm in a firm but gentle grip.

"What are you—" He stood so close. His irises captivated her. Brown with shots of yellow, and in the barn, just a hint of the glint predators got in the dark.

"Let me see your phone, Patience." His voice caressed over her and she almost reached into her pocket.

What was she doing? Clenching her fist, she gritted out a "No."

He cocked his head, but didn't release her. "You've been sneaking peeks at it all day. Makes me wonder who you contacted when you were driving back alone."

"I called my brother, okay?" She glared at him. It was the truth and the less she thought about the reason why she called him, the better. "I didn't want him to worry if he stops out. I don't usually bring strange men home, because believe me, the men I meet are strange."

His gaze hardened. "But you do bring men home?"

"A girl has her needs. I guess I could go to Razor's Edge—"

"You're not going anywhere near there."

She cocked a brow but didn't say anything.

"You're human," he said defensively.

"And humans and shifters don't..." She couldn't bring herself to finish the sentence. Not with him that close.

His lips thinned. "The crowd at Razor's Edge would eat you up and spit you out with no more than a single strand of meat on your bones."

He wanted to scare her, but the way he said it felt more like a promise. "I don't know." She shouldn't keep pushing him, but this topic pissed him off for some reason. "I've known several people who frequent there and do more than drink and play pool. They survived, and their stories, let me tell you—"

"You don't need to tell me anything," he gritted. "I'm fully aware of what it's like. Your phone."

She smiled slowly, only because she thought it might dig under his skin even more, letting him know that she'd won the Razor's Edge argument. His gaze sharpened and stole the breath from her lungs.

She backed up and his grip softened, but he followed her. She took another step. Her back hit the post that marked the edge of Dot's pen.

"Your. Phone. Patience."

"You have no right." It was useless, but she had to try. He'd barged into her life. And did a lot of work around her place...

He snaked his hand into the front pocket of her hoodie. She let out an indignant gasp but froze otherwise. His hand was big and so close, the flimsy fabric only amplifying the heat pouring off him.

If she had a heater like him in her bed during the winter, she'd never wake up cold. She'd never leave the bed.

A triumphant look crossed his face as he withdrew the phone. She scowled at him, then returned the triumphant grin when he glared at her lock screen.

He held it face-out toward her. "Unlock it."

"You would be able to see any new messages right there on the screen."

"Only the ones you haven't seen yet."

She narrowed her eyes, challenging him. After the years of stories she'd heard about shifters and their tempers and their viciousness, she shouldn't be provoking him. But she didn't feel one ounce of danger emanating from him.

He leaned in, dipping his head until his face hovered sinfully close to hers. "Do you want me to do that for you, too?"

Yes. She did. She wanted to see how far he'd take it.

She held his gaze, reached up, and typed her code in. There were easier ways, but she wasn't going the easy route with anything today.

He didn't move away when he scrolled through her contacts, looking at who she called and messaged.

Thankfully, her brother had been vague.

When Malcolm finished, he didn't hand her phone back. He slipped it back into her sweater and she sucked in a breath, which made her chest rise enough to touch him.

His gaze tracked over her face, brushing down her cheek to her lips. His pupils dilated and she had the strongest urge to lick her lips, just to see what he'd do, but afraid he'd do nothing but walk away.

"Patience?" A familiar voice rang out.

Malcolm spun around, blocking her like she was in danger from her own neighbor.

Oh, *shit*. Her neighbor. Her very shifter neighbor who knew that Patience knew about them and hadn't reported her.

HE HOVERED SO close to a bad decision. The interruption saved him. That didn't stop him from lifting his lip and sneering over his shoulder. Who the fuck blocked him before he touched paradise?

And could they wait to approach until his raging erection went down?

"Patience?" This time, the female was more concerned. The shifter female.

"My neighbor." Patience placed her hand on his back. He simultaneously wanted to jerk away and lean into her. Her touch wasn't hesitant, but full of warning. She was trying to talk him and his bared canines down while reassuring him that she wasn't in danger and that the approaching shifter wasn't a danger.

The latter he wasn't so sure about. With him, her neighbor might react differently.

"Whoa, Delia. Just wait." Another shifter. Male this time, and more cautious.

"I'm in the barn," Patience called. Her hand remained on him. "They're my friends," she whispered.

But they weren't his. He didn't have friends.

That last thought deepened his scowl. Where did that come from? He had... Well, the other Guardians were more like coworkers, and he only socialized with Harrison, and only when they were looking to get laid. Other than that? No one.

"Are you alone?" Delia called cautiously.

Malcolm sensed the male circling around the back of the barn. They sensed him here and their worry drifted in on the light breeze.

"No, I'm with a...guy."

The male rounded the door that led to the goat pen. The goats were as calm as they'd been around him. They were familiar with the male. "Are you sure you're all right?"

Delia flanked the front. Malcolm resisted the urge to crowd Patience more than he already was. He'd press her into the wall if he got any closer.

"She's fine," he said.

Before he could say anything else, Patience slipped out from behind him and pasted a smile on her face. "This is Malcolm. We met last night and he's been helping me around the place."

Neither shifter relaxed. This wasn't really a scenario they could play along to. They knew what he was, and he knew what they were—and that Patience knew about them all. Pretending any different would be foolish, so he said, "Could I talk to you two privately?"

Patience spun on him, her blue eyes spitting fire. "Why?"

"It's all right, Patience," Delia said softly while warily eyeing him. "I think a talk would be a good idea."

She wanted Patience away from him. They were doing it for her protection. It was the only reason he wasn't growling.

Patience made a disgruntled noise and stomped out of the barn. It took more effort than he ever would've thought not to watch her round ass sway underneath that bulky, dirty sweater. She was a leggings girl and he hoped she never changed.

He steadied his gaze on the neighbors. "How about we start with names." They were still trying to flank him, but he wasn't concerned. Two civilians wouldn't be a fair match against a Guardian. Then again, he didn't have his brother for backup since he technically wasn't supposed to be working.

Yeah, he'd have to call his boss about all this.

"You first," the male said. He was shorter than Malcolm, but still over six feet tall. The female stood a few inches shorter than the other male. These two were mates. Other than that, Malcolm didn't detect much beyond their fondness for Patience.

"Malcolm." He glanced at the female. Her flaxen hair was in a messy bun, and her blue jeans were as dusty as his pants. Same with the male. They must've walked from their place.

"As I'm sure you've already heard, I'm Delia." She lifted her chin to her mate. "And he's Brenden. Why are you with Patience?"

Telling them the real story would undermine his authority if they knew what a bad way Patience found him in.

A limited version of the truth was best. Any sense of a lie wouldn't earn their trust. "I'm on a vacation of sorts and we crossed paths last night after I had a little too much to drink."

Delia sighed. "That's Patience for you. Always with the rescuing."

"Why are you still here?" Brenden's tone sounded partially hostile and somewhat curious. "She has nothing to offer you."

Only witty conversation, a parcel of land full of opportunities and distractions from what's been gnawing at him, and a body that gave him the strongest erection he could remember. "I could tell she knew about our kind."

"So? She's harmless," Delia said.

"It's not allowed."

Brenden's hostility inflated. "Well, it's not your job—"

"It is. I might be on leave, but I can't exactly ignore something like this. I'm a Guardian."

Silence. The two exchanged looks and were likely mind-speaking with each other. Malcolm's skin tingled with the energy and he stomped down his envy. Harrison and Malcolm didn't need to mind-speak. They worked as one. It was like their own little superpower. But those who worked closely together could often mind-speak.

And so could mates. He came up short on both accounts.

Delia kicked her chin up. "Then you're going to have to punish the whole damn town. All the shifters around here know about her and don't give a damn. She's a good person."

The whole damn town?

"You mean…all the shifters in and around Twin Forks know that Patience and her brother know about shifters?"

Brenden hissed out a breath.

Yep, Malcolm knew about the brother. This problem was growing bigger for all involved. It was possible that the Synod would overlook the transgression, but they'd still vote to wipe the humans' minds. It was safer for all of them.

"Everyone that I know. You can't mix in a town this small and not get assholes that'd take advantage of humans. Twin Forks is mostly human, and the shifter colonies nearby keep to themselves, but there's a few who've found workarounds to fool humans when we don't continue to age and they do, or they just move away. It's safer for Patience and Jacob to know about us. Then they can steer clear."

But Patience steered toward him and not away. Because she didn't know what he was at first. If he was a bastard, he could've used her ignorance to his advantage. He could've robbed her, killed her, or…seduced her.

Delia's point wasn't lost on him. Didn't mean that he could ignore his job. "What other humans in Twin Forks know about us?"

Delia shrugged. "I don't interact with anyone but Patience, and her brother if he's out for a visit. Brenden and I have lived here for a few decades and it's the same every time. They grow old and die. We'd rather not bury friends over and over again."

But it was hard to avoid neighbors. "How do you stay hidden?"

Brenden answered. "I can make us look older in the

humans' minds. If we run across an elderly couple, they think I'm the son of Brenden Anderson Senior and what a coincidence, I also married a Delia."

A nice ability to have. Most shifters had their own special ability that contributed to the shifter world or made it easier to live among humans. He wished more shifters had Brenden's ability.

Malcolm only had the twin thing. Since Harrison lived with Sylva in another colony hundreds of miles away, Malcolm was in the middle of nowhere with no backup and no special ability.

He'd rather have the neighbors on his side. "Look, I don't want anything bad to happen to Patience. But you understand that I've got to report her and Jacob." He should meet Jacob soon. Was he as reliable as Patience seemed? That'd help their case. "I plan to stick around until this is settled." He gestured to the wheelbarrow. "Don't worry, I'm earning my keep."

Delia crossed her arms. "That's not the only issue." Her mate shot her a warning look and Malcolm sensed more mental speak. "Patience isn't immune to our...heightened sexual needs." Her jaw clenched, but she leveled her accusatory stare on him. "And she's attracted to you."

"I don't plan on hurting her," he said, too aware that he wasn't promising not to touch her. The words wouldn't come out.

"You will if your commander or the Synod orders it," Brenden said.

"They won't order anything more than a mind wipe." He could probably do that on his own. He didn't work with humans much, and cleaning their presence from a human's mind was like a muscle that most shifters would rather avoid using. Patience's knowledge was extensive, going back years. If he fucked up, he could leave her with damaging memory loss. Yet, he didn't want another shifter looking deep into her light blue eyes and tampering with that sharp mind.

"We don't know that yet, do we?" Delia said quietly. "You said you'd be here 'earning your keep' while waiting for the orders. Patience doesn't get attention from males like you."

He was glad to hear it, but his inner wolf raged. Who wouldn't appreciate her quiet beauty and sarcastic remarks? Idiots. All of them. "Who does she get attention from?"

Brenden snorted. "The psycho stalker was probably the best-looking of the bunch, but most guys she dates are more like a man-child . Maybe you should get a hotel room."

Not happening. "And give her a chance to hide more from me? No."

The two exchanged another look before Delia spoke. "If you fuck with her, we're going to tear you limb from limb. We can hide in these trees so well, an entire pack could search for us and never find a thing."

Malcolm's mind transported him back to the year after his sister disappeared. No sign. No scent. No tracks. His sister disappeared, and he and Harrison scoured the woods around his colony until they nearly went insane.

Giving himself a mental shake, he concentrated on the moment. "I'll take the chance."

CHAPTER 5

*H*e was still here. Only he wasn't snoozing on her couch.

Patience descended the stairs after a night of fitful sleep, her nose guiding her to the savory smells wafting from the kitchen. A pile of blankets was folded neatly by the couch.

How long had he been up?

After Delia and Brenden left with strict instructions to call—or shout and scream—and they'd come running, she went inside to take a long bath. She managed not to interact with Malcolm too much for the rest of the night.

He searched through her grandma's things, and as much as she wanted to go out to the garage and see him combing through Grandma's miniature doll collection with his big hands, she stayed in and watched TV.

She might have to re-watch all the shows from last night. Long stretches would go by and she'd realize that she hadn't been paying attention, wondering about what Malcolm and her neighbors talked about and what he found in the garage.

Nothing that would interest him. She knew that much.

Good thing he met Delia and Brenden instead of the mate

of Brenden's late brother. She was toxic, a female who thrilled in the possibility of getting outed by living in town, and loved treating people like shit.

Patience rounded the corner into her kitchen and steeled herself against the sight of Malcolm and his rock-hard body and those lips that twisted when he caught her in an almost-lie, like he enjoyed this game of cat and mouse.

Only, it felt more like wolf and rabbit.

No amount of titanium in her spine could've prepared her for a shirtless Malcolm frying eggs at her stove. He wore blue jeans today. Rugged, worn, they hugged his hips and molded around his strong thighs.

This was the only time in her life she thought she should've dressed up for breakfast. She wore yesterday's outfit of pajama pants, a T-shirt, and her pink fluffy robe. She didn't look like him when she cooked the eggs the day before.

He glanced over his shoulder, the muscles of his back rippling as he worked the spatula. "Good morning, sleepyhead."

"Don't tell me you wake at the crack of dawn."

He got a wicked glint in his eye and his voice did that low rumble that went straight to the naughtiest parts of her imagination. "If I'm not already up."

Some sort of undignified grunt left her and she trudged to the fridge. Good thing she didn't have her heart set on seducing him. One, she didn't have a seductive bone in her body. And two, she doubted he'd be interested in nothing more than a roll in the hay.

Besides, having sex in hay was not romantic. Her high school boyfriend taught her that before he left town and insinuated she was a loser for not moving away from Twin Forks.

She snagged the orange juice from the fridge. "You don't have to cook."

"I might have forced myself in, but I don't have to be rude."

"Your mama taught you better than that?"

He snorted. "Not my Maw. She'd probably get cigarette ash all over your carpet and cuss you sideways for mentioning anything."

He didn't sound like there were any hard feelings. He acted more nostalgic than anything.

"She wasn't a nurturer?" she asked.

"No. She let us run wild."

"You and your brother."

His shoulders tightened and his focus lasered on the frying pan. "And my sister."

She didn't need superhuman senses to know something was wrong there. "I'm sorry," she said softly.

He took the pan off the stove and plopped it on a hot pad. He stared at it for a moment. She thought he'd brush it all off and change the subject, but he didn't. "She went missing. A long time ago."

"Just like that?"

He nodded.

"That's horrible." And really hard to do in their world.

"Yeah. It was. No blood trail, no scent, and no signs. Harrison and I tracked her for a year and couldn't find anything."

Her skin prickled. That sounded way too familiar. It sounded deliberate. Was his sister abducted...or had she left on her own? She couldn't think too hard on that and risk him sensing something she couldn't hide. "What was her name?"

"Camille. It was just a bad time. All of it."

She tried to play it casual and peeked under a napkin

draped over a plate. A pile of pancakes. Her stomach rumbled, but she kept Malcolm talking as long as he was willing. If he was combing through her life, she got to learn about him, too. "Were you pretty young when it happened?"

"For a shifter? Yes. For a human, too. Harrison and I hadn't left home yet, and it's not like many shifters went to college then. We were kicking around our land, freeloading for a while, trying to delay the inevitable of going to Guardian training." He turned and leaned against her Formica counter. "And our mates were there."

Her brows rose and her jaw dropped. She snapped it shut. He had a mate?

He shook his head, reading her unspoken question. "No, I'm not mated. Mine chose to be with someone else and leave the pack, and Harrison's was killed while we were searching for Camille."

"Oh, Malcolm. I'm sorry." Each was devastating in its own way. She didn't only see the bad side of mating and marriage and relationships through her work, but she was surrounded by enough stable couples to see what a deep and lasting connection they'd made.

She jokingly blamed Delia and Brenden on her failed dates. If they weren't so connected, so loyal, and so devoted to each other, Patience might've settled for much less long ago.

Malcolm took two plates out of the drying rack and dished up their food. "I got over it. It's better she left me before we mated. After we bonded, it would've been impossible."

She bit the inside of her lip, not trusting herself to say anything. Who wouldn't want Malcolm? "Looks good."

He glanced up, his eyes narrowing. She hoped he assumed her reaction wasn't from any awkwardness in the conversation.

She took her plate to the table and sat. "What's on your agenda for today?"

He took the seat across from her. "What do you need to get done?"

"Chores. And I have a batch of goat-milk soap to make." If he was going to offer his services, he could stir. It was the most tedious part of soap making.

"That's all the supplies in the basement?"

He'd been down there too? "Yes. I have a few batches curing."

"Do you sell it?"

"No. I work at a women's shelter and we use plenty there. Otherwise, there's always someplace I can donate it to."

"Homemade goat-milk soap could fetch a premium price." His gaze appraised her.

She shoved her eggs around on the plate. "I have a roof over my head I didn't have to pay for, and a good job despite not having a college education. I'm fortunate enough in life. I don't have to sell the soap when I got the goats for free."

Though she could use the money. There were repairs to make inside and out of her home. What extra money she did have went to the chickens and the goats. It never failed that when she felt like she'd gotten ahead for once, one of her cats or dogs needed vet attention.

"Truthfully," she said, "I've been known to barter a batch or two for rabies vaccinations."

"Oof." He gave an exaggerated wince. "Selfish much?"

She chuckled and stuffed a forkful of pancake into her mouth. The fluffy bite dissolved into an orgasm for her tongue. She moaned. "Oh my gosh. Where did you learn to make pancakes like this?"

He swallowed, his gaze glued to her mouth. She averted her eyes and took another bite. He clocked her every move.

"Harrison and I have been on our own for a while. And Maw's a mean bastard, but she can cook."

His description of his mom made her snort around her mouthful. No one ever accused her of being too ladylike. "She and my grandma might've gotten along or been bitter enemies."

He gave her a small smile. "Maw doesn't have friends, but she's solid in the bitter enemies category. So, my pancakes have the Patience Montgomery stamp of approval?"

She rolled her eyes. "It's not a very distinguished honor."

"My pancakes say it is." He'd already finished his food and she had barely touched her plate. "May I use your bathroom?"

"I dunno. You gonna search my bedroom without asking?"

"Would it be better if you knew I was doing it?"

Her cheeks flamed. She didn't think she had anything scandalous and embarrassing. She wasn't one for sex toys and lingerie. She'd probably be more ashamed about the lack of anything incriminating he'd find.

But Malcolm searching through her underwear drawer might be more than her heart could take.

"I'm undecided," she finally said.

"I'll surprise you." He left the kitchen. His footsteps up the stairs sounded surprisingly light for such a large guy.

She finished her plate and began dishes. It was the first time she'd done any since Malcolm arrived, not that she usually tackled them after every meal. But he did. Since he had cooked, she did.

He moved around her place like he'd been staying here a while. It'd been about twenty-four hours since she'd met him and she already knew she'd miss having him around.

WHEN HE HEARD the water kick on in the kitchen, he made his call. He could speak low enough for his boss to hear him, but since the bathroom was right outside of Patience's bedroom and she was still in her pink robe, he had to be quick.

He'd showered last night so he wouldn't track dust all over the house, but Patience must've been asleep by then.

He also should've made his phone call last night while she slept. Or when she was in the house and he was in the garage.

But her life fascinated him. To be honest, the garage wasn't *her* life. It was her grandma's and an accumulation of the woman's entire history. Why hadn't Patience gone through any of it? Were the collections too personal? There were miniature figurines, porcelain dolls, jewelry boxes—all filled with costume jewelry. He also found boxes of embroidered handkerchiefs and enough dishtowels—also all with embroidery—to keep Twin Forks drying dishes for many years.

And there were the pictures. Only one plastic bin full, but he'd looked through them all. He knew what Patience's brother and parents looked like, but there weren't any pictures of her mom or dad beyond when Patience was a baby.

The mom, he knew why. A cutout of her obituary and her funeral program was in storage, along with the grandma's. But nothing for the dad. Where was his?

Commander Fitzsimmons answered. "I didn't expect to hear from you for a while."

"Yeah, well, my travels landed me in a place that made me put my Guardian hat back on." He explained the story, grimacing over the part of him being in the middle of nowhere and unconscious.

"So, this Patience has known about us for most of her life, if she's to be believed, and hasn't told anyone?"

"Same with her brother. I haven't met him yet."

The other end grew quiet. As oddly protective as Malcolm was starting to feel over Patience, he trusted Commander Fitzsimmons to think through the problem. He wouldn't be heavy-handed unless the situation called for it.

"If they've known about us that long," Commander Fitzsimmons said, "A few more days won't hurt. Follow your gut. You think there's more to the story, then there probably is. And…" His pause sent zaps of tension through his body. "Once you think you know the extent of it, we'll have to take care of it. This occurrence might be harmless, but we can't let them set a precedent."

Otherwise, the human mate of so-and-so would think it was okay to tell her family, and word would spread until eventually their kind was outed. Malcolm pinched the bridge of his nose. He'd do what he had to do. But wiping Patience's sharp mind would be a dark blotch in his career.

"Need backup?" The commander's question yanked Malcolm out of his thoughts.

"No." He spoke so fast he hadn't had time to consider whether he really needed backup. "Let me check around first. Twin Forks is small enough that I might draw more attention now than from what I did at Razor's Edge. It'll be worse if there's more of us."

"Sounds like you needed something like this, just for a while," his commander said, more benign than Malcolm had ever heard him talk. They didn't have to be face-to-face for the male to sense the turmoil over the connection. "But we've got Guardians in the field, and of course Harrison can find you easier than anyone. Don't hesitate to call."

"Got it."

He hung up in time to catch the faint buzz of an engine. Someone else coming?

Did she normally get that many visitors?

He peeked out the window, knowing damn well that it didn't face the drive into her yard but toward the back of the house. He caught the glint of a vehicle on the road through the trees surrounding her place.

Waiting in the bathroom, he cracked the door. Patience was singing off-tune to herself, oblivious to the impending arrival. She moved around downstairs. The dishes were done. She must be getting those obnoxious but cute yellow boots on and finding another oversized sweater to throw on instead of her robe.

A car door shut, but Patience's singing continued.

The doorbell rang. She cut off and didn't move. Was she not expecting company, or afraid for her visitor because he was here?

He leaned out farther.

"Damian, what do you want?"

Her shouted question made his frown deepen. She hadn't even opened the door.

"I saw you in town," came a muffled reply. "I was worried."

"Because I was in town?" Scorn dripped from her tone.

Malcolm concluded two things: this was an unexpected visit and she didn't like her visitor. He drifted down the stairs.

"You were with a guy," Damian called. "You looked scared. Talk to me, Patience. Are you all right?"

"That's none of your business. Not about how I'm doing or about who I'm with."

"He was really scary, honey. Come on, open up. I'm concerned."

Honey? Malcolm's canines pulsed. He wanted to rip into

something, preferably the jugular of the guy who called Patience *honey*.

"Of all the…" Patience muttered. "Does Brenden need to talk to you again or should I go get that restraining order?"

Restraining order. Brenden's comment about a psycho stalker wasn't an exaggeration.

Malcolm pounded down the rest of the stairs. Patience jumped, managing to cut off a shout. This Damian's arrival had her all wound up.

"Patience?" Damian banged on the door. The flimsy wood rattled. If he kept it up, the door would crumble. "Open up."

Patience's eyes were wide as she watched him storm across the living room to the entry. He whipped open the door and caught Damian's fist mid-knock. He held tight, his grip punishing.

Damian's eyes went wider than Patience's and the color drained from his face. His mouth dropped open, but no sound came out.

"Patience, *honey*," Malcolm said through gritted teeth. "Mind telling this dickwad exactly how scared I make you?"

He had to give her plenty of credit. She didn't miss a beat and scurried over to him. She tucked herself under the arm holding the door and clung to his waist. Her other hand rested on his abdomen.

"Damian, this is Malcolm. He's staying here."

He dropped his hand off the door and wrapped it around her shoulders. Damian tugged futilely on his arm, but Malcolm didn't release him until he quit trying, then he tossed it away from him like a piece of garbage.

Damian curled his hand into his chest. Color returned to his cheeks and indignation rose in his dark eyes. "He's living with you?"

"Got a problem with that?" Malcolm snapped.

Damian flinched and his hand balled into a fist again.

Malcolm studied him. The possessive look the human got when his gaze landed on Patience was sick, like the kind of possession where he'd end up killing her, stuffing her body, and posing her with the dolls in the garage.

"Y-yes," Damian stammered. "Patience doesn't have men over, and she's not dating anyone, so I don't believe she's acting of her own free will."

Patience made a choking sound. Malcolm didn't know if that was because Damian had ironically nailed the situation, or if she was pissed that he didn't believe her and was still trying to save her.

Malcolm leaned closer, taking Patience with him, mostly because he didn't want to let her go. "Have you been watching her?"

Guilt flashed in the man's eyes. Busted. Rage boiled under Malcolm's skin. This pervert had been spying on Patience.

He had to be dealt with. And as much as Malcolm wanted to use one well-aimed punch to put the man out of his misery, he couldn't.

"Wait here," he murmured to Patience and stepped out the door.

Damian stumbled back. The man stood only a few inches shorter than him and fit Brenden's description of being good-looking enough, which irritated him more.

Malcolm clapped his hand on Damian's shoulder and steered him off the porch. Tripod snarled at the human. When Damian kicked his foot out, Malcolm tightened his grip enough to drop the man to his knees.

"Hurt any of these animals and I'll do the same to you tenfold."

"O-okay. Sorry."

Yanking him to his feet, Malcolm pushed him forward. Damian spun around, already spewing some kind of entitled nonsense, but Malcolm caught him by the chin and looked deep into his eyes.

Damian's brow furrowed but he didn't look away.

Calling on his rusty skills of mind manipulation, he didn't worry about using a deft touch. Anything and everything with Patience, he wiped, including her brother and the neighbors. He buried the memories so deep, a neurosurgeon could hunt for centuries and not find them.

Damian's eyes rolled back and a moan escaped him. His knees buckled until he hung from Malcolm's unrelenting grip.

Malcolm released his hand and the man crumbled to the ground.

"Oh my gosh." Patience rushed out but didn't go to Damian's side. She peered over him like he was a science experiment. "Did you kill him?"

"Would you mind if I did?"

"I feel like my real answer would make me look bad."

He chuffed out a laugh. Never what he expected. "No, but he shouldn't remember anything about you."

"Whoa. Really?"

He inclined his head, refraining from saying more about it.

"Can you all do that?"

He shouldn't answer. She knew way too much as it was. "Somewhat. It's a survival mechanism. But it's still an exposure risk so we have, like, a natural aversion to doing it. I think because we're taught when we're young to avoid risking exposure altogether."

"Makes sense."

It should feel wrong talking to a human about his kind, not freeing. "I need to know where he lives so I can drive his car back, tuck him in, and let him think he went to bed hours ago with a whopping migraine."

"I'm going with you."

He was going to sneak an unconscious man into a house in broad daylight, and then walk miles back. That wasn't a problem for him. For her, it was different. "Not a good idea."

"Malcolm. This guy has stalked me for a year and a half. I've come home to him doing my chores and scaring Dot. He's kicked my dogs. He's shown up at work and terrified some of the women I help. And he's cock-blocked me on more than one occasion."

Her nostrils were flaring and her hands were stuffed into the soft pink fabric at her hips.

He should've gone easier on Damian for the cock-blocking service. Those guys probably weren't good enough for Patience either.

"I have no idea why he fixated on me. There are enough single beautiful women that haven't left Twin Forks yet." She stomped back to the house. "I'm getting dressed. Don't you dare leave, or I'll just follow you."

Malcolm's lips twitched. He gazed down at Damian.

Patience might not understand why she was a target, but he did. She had a big heart and was sexy in an understated way. Any guy would be lucky to be allowed to spend his life with her, and Damian wanted to be that guy. The only problem was that she didn't want him. She'd rightfully sensed the dangerous edge of his attention.

Damian needed mental help. A lot of it. But that wasn't Malcolm's job.

Patience was his job and he was more than happy to focus on her.

CHAPTER 6

There was never a point in her life when she would've believed someone who told her that one day, she'd be tucking an unconscious stalker into bed and doing it with the hottest guy she'd ever laid eyes on. Or that the hot guy was willing to help her out of a situation that she only saw escalating to a point where the only end was incarceration or death—hers or Damian's.

They stood back. Malcolm had loaded Damian into the back seat of his car. He'd driven while she followed and gave directions over the phone. Then she parked a few blocks away and hopped in with him. She'd never been so thankful for an attached garage and a remote entry. Damian had both.

She looked at Malcolm's strong profile scowling at the bed. "Are you sure he won't remember me?"

"Pretty sure."

"I guess it's better than nothing. I suppose we can walk back to my car. Do we have to sneak out the back or something?"

"I'll check our surroundings, and if no one's outside or

peering out their window, we should be fine to just walk out."

And if anyone asked Damian about his visitors, he'd be confused and maybe get a headache? She didn't know and didn't care, as long as he forgot her.

Malcolm looked around the surprisingly stylish room with earth tone paint and dark blinds and quality wood furniture. "At least there's no murder board with your picture all over it."

"Well, we haven't seen the basement. I heard his last girl-friend took out a restraining order, too. Of course, I heard that after I'd already been out with him and gave him the thanks-but-no-thanks talk."

"Did you tell him it was him and not you?"

She snickered. "I almost went out with him again. Most of the men I meet in the area think that because I'm not next in line to be a Victoria's Secret model I should be grateful for their attention. And that it's a sin that I don't care to date them even though I'm already thirty-two."

"Human men are often intimidated by a strong woman."

She answered without thinking. "So are shifter males."

He shot her a look that said *What are you talking about?* but then he looked away, his gaze troubled. "I guess, yeah. Some are assholes." His brow furrowed like he was still considering her comment, but all he said was, "We'd better get going."

She'd gotten him thinking, and after years of hearing how terrifying Guardians were, she didn't expect him to not at least argue about it for a while. Were the others like him, or did fate drop this one in particular in her ditch?

They stepped outside and walked down the sidewalk like they didn't have a care in the world. This might be a normal occurrence for Malcolm, but she had a hard time not looking behind her, waiting for someone to shout at them, asking what the hell they did to Damian.

"It's okay, Patience," Malcolm said.

If shifters' senses were really that enhanced, her anxiety must be billowing around her like a mushroom cloud. She concentrated on even breathing.

Malcolm peered around. They were a block away from her vehicle. "Is this the same area we drove through yesterday?"

She lifted her chin toward the main road that cut through Damian's residential neighborhood. "That's the one we took home from Razor's Edge."

His gaze swept over the small homes, his lips turned down.

She was about to ask him if something was wrong, when the voice she hated hearing the most pierced the peaceful neighborhood.

"Mal?"

Patience kept walking, glad that Tamera didn't say her name, until it dawned on her…Tamera knew Malcolm?

Patience twisted to find Malcolm frozen in place, a haunted expression plastered on his face.

Tamera stood on the other side of the street, at the corner. What epically shitty luck that Tamera lived close to Damian. Why couldn't Damian stalk someone like her? He'd get chewed up and spit out and be too terrified to do it again.

Tamera's bright golden eyes ate up Malcolm's body. When she'd devoured her fill, she flicked an irritated glance toward Patience. Her eyes lit and a seductive sneer crossed her face. "*Ho-ly* shit. That *is* you. And with a hu—with our dear Patience. I figured it was only time before our paths crossed again."

"Tam," Malcolm croaked.

Ugh. These two had nicknames for each other? She edged toward her car, hoping Malcolm would sense her and follow.

But he stood rooted in place, his fists clenching and unclenching.

Tamera floated across the road, uncaring of whether there was traffic or not. Too bad there wasn't. The female could use a dent to her ego by an old rickety clunker.

She'd piled her rich blond hair on top of her head and her hips swayed in her designer jeans with each step. She held her arms out. "Is that how you greet me after all these years?"

Patience took another step farther away.

The move didn't escape Tamera's notice. "Look at Rescue Rabbit, running away," she purred. She wrapped her arms around Malcolm and plastered her willowy body against him.

Panic lit his eyes but he didn't move. Neither did he hug her back.

"How you doing, baby?" Tamera drawled and kissed his cheek, lingering much longer than a typical friend would.

Either the endearment or the kiss brought him back into focus, but he continued to be stuck in her snare. "Good. And…you?"

She kept her arms draped over his shoulders and cocked one voluptuous hip. Why couldn't someone so ugly inside be the same outside?

"I heard the rumors at Razor's Edge about a new arrival, leaving his partners wanting so bad that they had to fuck three other males just to make it go away. They said he couldn't perform, or he wouldn't. That could *not* be you, could it?"

Malcolm grimaced and a pink tint suffused his cheeks.

Was he blushing?

"It was just a… I didn't mean to…" He snapped his mouth shut.

His expression looked so tortured that Patience wanted to jump in and help him, but had no idea how. Her run-ins with Tamera usually ended up with a smirking Tamera while she was flayed open. The female was a truffle pig for insecurities.

"Now I can see why you're with Rescue Rabbit." She dropped her voice to a theatrical whisper. "She won't be too much for you. She probably hasn't been touched in so long she'll go off like—"

"Oh, no. We aren't together. Like that."

Patience recoiled. He'd been so quick to jump to her defense when Damian stood at the door, but it was open season around Tamera?

Tamera cupped his face, still pressed against him. "Baby, it's no big deal. A guy like you has to play. You should let me know when you need it next. I don't smell like a chicken coop."

Patience bit the inside of her cheek. It never helped to say anything.

Malcolm shrugged out of the female's hold, shaking his head. "Um, no, but uh…thanks anyway." His expression appeared more dazed now. "What about Darius?"

It was the first time since Patience had known Tamera that she saw actual grief. The female sniffled and averted her gaze. "He had to be a hero and volunteer on the rural fire department." She rolled her lips in, her eyes shimmering. "He's no longer with us. Forest fire."

"I'm sorry," Malcolm said woodenly as if the information hadn't sunk in yet.

What was their story? She'd be more sympathetic but…it was Tamera.

As if to make up for the slip in her meanness, Tamera pinned her with a predatory gaze and wrinkled her nose. "Rabbit, I think there's a little goat poop stuck to your shoe."

Patience gave her a flat stare. Tamera said something similar each time they crossed paths, but Patience had enough compassion to let it pass. Losing Darius had to have been hard. She'd heard shifter mates couldn't survive when one passed. Tamara must have done it out of sheer meanness.

Malcolm was shuffling to the car, getting closer to Patience but not looking at her.

"What are you doing in town?" Tamera asked, shoving her hands in her back pockets, which only meant her generous breasts stuck out even farther.

"Business," he mumbled.

"With Rescue Rabbit?" The curiosity was the only thing genuine about Tamera.

Patience had long given up on asking her not to call her that. And it apparently didn't faze Malcolm.

"How's Harrison?" The blond advanced, not letting them go.

Patience wanted to leave, to ditch Malcolm on the sidewalk and save herself, but she stayed.

"Mated," Malcolm answered.

Patience blinked at him. He was reduced to one-word replies. Her witty, self-deprecating shifter was struck dumb by Tamera.

Tamera's eyes flared, but she covered her surprise with false sympathy. "I heard how you two did *everything* together. Does he share his mate, too?"

Malcolm shook his head, his distaste for Tamera's suggestion apparent. "No."

"Oh, my poor Mal. Is that why you're here, settling for Rescue Rabbit instead of finding yourself someone to mate with? Your twin has someone else?"

His jaw clenched and the Malcolm that Patience knew, for albeit a short while, returned. "No, Tam. I'm not looking to mate anyone. We had that chance and you chose Darius."

❧

THE FROSTY RIDE back to Patience's place didn't help Malcolm's mindset.

Tamera.

His *mate,* Tamera.

Was that why he was drawn to bumfuck Twin Forks during his slow mental breakdown? Did their old connection somehow roar to life and draw him here just to make him suffer?

He had no idea her mate perished. But she'd certainly heard enough about him.

There was a time when she was everything to him. He'd been determined to have a different relationship than his parents had, a loving one that went beyond sheer loyalty and was caring and compassionate.

Tamera had taken that away from him. Yes, some shifters moved on and found others to mate, but it wasn't simple. It wasn't like human marriage and *until death do us part.* Mating lasted for eternity, and the soul-deep connection was so strong once they were officially mated, that when one died, the other often did, too.

But Tamera was alive and well.

She looked the same, all blond bombshell. Her personality was... Damn, had she been that cutting all those years ago?

Patience stayed quiet the entire drive. She pulled onto the parking pad outside of the garage and killed the engine. She was about to leave without saying a word when he asked the first thing that came to mind, just to end the silence.

"What's the deal with Rescue Rabbit?"

Patience's withering look would've shriveled a lesser male. "It's a derogatory name your girlfriend calls me because she knows I hate it."

"She's not my girlfriend." What was Tamera to him? An ex? She'd been nothing but phantom pain for so long, he hadn't been prepared to see her in person. And then learn that she was unmated.

"Well, you made it clear I'm not, either." She got out and slammed the door, making his ears ring from the noise.

What the hell?

He got out. "What's that supposed to mean? Was I supposed to lie to her?"

Patience shook her head before she turned around. "Never mind. It's none of my business. You're probably going to end up doing whatever mind trick that you did to Damian to me when all this is over. She's your mate and all, so it's not my business."

"She's not my mate. She picked Darius."

Patience flung her hand up and twirled it in the air as she continued to the barn. "Good news! She's single now. I'm surprised you didn't run into her the other night."

He meant to go after her, but he paused. What would have happened if he had? Would he have succumbed, fucked around with her, then doggedly tried to win her back? How long had she been mourning a mate?

Numbness settled over him. His mate was single again.

Did he feel anything for her?

A bleat snapped him back to the present. Patience was in the barn. She hadn't gotten chores done this morning before Damian pounded on her door.

He jogged to the barn. "What can I help with?"

Dot was munching on grain and Patience's ass was planted on an upside-down five-gallon bucket next to the goat, her mouth set in a mutinous line. "Nothing. I'm sure you have work to do."

He didn't claim to have an inside track on how women think, but her mood was clear. "You're upset with me."

"Why would I be?"

He grabbed another bucket and tipped it over. Dropping

down on it, he rested his elbows on his knees. He felt like he should explain—everything. No one knew the story except for his family, and the rest of the pack he grew up with probably figured it out. But he'd never told it out loud.

"You know how mates work?"

She shrugged. "Somewhat."

"You know we live for a while, for centuries even?"

She nodded, her hands working the teats. Dot was happy with her food and barely noticed them.

He took a deep breath. "Shifters usually meet their mates later. They have a chance to sow their wild oats and all that." She rolled her eyes, but he kept going. "A mating bond, when vows are said and blood is exchanged with a dagger we call a gladdus, is a soul-deep connection, so deep that when one dies, the other often follows."

"Then how could Tamera choose another?"

He lifted a shoulder. "I wondered the same thing for so many years. Tam and I grew up in the same colony. Which means after puberty ended, we sensed that we belonged with each other. I came from a good family. Sure, my Maw is bat shit and my father is ambivalent at best, but otherwise, I could've given her a normal shifter life. Well, normal for a Guardian. Our life was set."

"But she felt differently," Patience said quietly.

"I guess she did. She mated Darius instead. She didn't just run off to mess around for a few years. That would've hurt, but I think I would've understood." Would he have? How often had he wondered that? He didn't think he would've forced Tamera into a mating she wasn't ready for.

He'd begged her not to bond herself with another. *Begged*.

Patience finished with Dot and moved the pail to a spot where it wouldn't get tipped. She faced him. "I can't pretend to comprehend how much bigger of a deal what she did is over a girl running off to marry somewhere else. But... I mean, was she different then?"

"Was she less of a bitch?"

Her head bobbed as she released Dot from her milking stall. "Yeah. Because you seemed fine with her insults and her overt come-ons, so that tells me maybe she isn't so different than the Tamera you knew. It makes me wonder how well this mating bond matches shifters, or if you're just the type that thinks it's okay because she's hot."

She grabbed the handle and stomped through the barn, stopping long enough to splash some milk into the cats' and dogs' bowl. They were lined up, waiting for their treat.

He was so close that when she spun around, she had to pull to a stop. Milk sloshed in the pail. She glowered at him.

"I've been wondering the same thing. She seemed more toxic than before. But if you knew my Maw—"

"I'd rather not. If she's anything like Tamera, believe me, I'd rather not."

Tamera and Maw were awfully similar now that he thought about it. If he brought home a human mate, Maw would go nuclear. She was a shifter and proud of it. She'd lorded her mate's station with their government over the rest of the pack before it was overthrown.

Patience tried to side-step him, but he was quick enough to keep her from escaping. "I feel like I did something wrong. Talk to me, Patience."

She considered him for a moment, her stare so hard it regressed him several decades until he felt like a squirmy kid again. "I'm pissed that you didn't jump in to help me like you did with Damian, and I'm even more pissed that I expected you to, and that I'm so terribly disappointed you didn't. I can take care of myself. I shouldn't be expecting anyone else to, especially not you."

"Why not me?" The main reason why he was still at her

place evaded him. All he could think about was that she'd trusted him and he let her down. "I'm sorry. The shock was… I never expected to see her again."

"Well, you did. Congratulations. You have your mate back."

She sidled around him and he let her go, his gaze dropping to the animals lapping up their milk. They were oblivious to his inner turmoil.

You have your mate back.

He should be overjoyed, but seeing Tamera didn't fill him with that sense of connection like it used to. In his mind, she was still someone else's mate.

He jogged after Patience. "Listen. I'm sorry, okay."

She shook her head. "Like I said, it's not your place to defend me. I've been enduring that woman and her caustic comments for years."

"Years?"

Her gaze landed on him and drifted away. "She had the grace to wait until I was over eighteen before ridiculing me."

"How have you crossed paths with her so often?"

"Darius was Brenden's brother."

He stopped. The neighbor? He hurried to catch back up to Patience. "Small world," he muttered.

"Big enough for her to leave now that she doesn't have Darius to make her look like she's aging to other people since he had the same ability as Brenden. Townsfolk are already starting to talk. I keep hoping each year is the one she'll have to move. She's looked twenty-five since I've known her."

It wasn't a good sign that humans were noticing her youthful glow, but females tended to get away with that longer than males.

He followed her into the house, dreading the possibility he or one of his fellow Guardians would have to force

Tamera to move to protect their kind. She never liked to be told what to do.

Patience plopped the bucket on the table and dug several ice cube trays out of a cupboard.

How did he find everything she did fascinating? "Milk ice?"

"When I make soap, the lye heats it up so bad that it can scorch it. So it helps when the milk is frozen. Then the temperature doesn't get quite that high."

"Huh." They were an isolated people, but he never recalled thinking about soap. If Maw made it, it'd probably have cigarette ash sprinkled all over it. He and Harrison usually took a dip in the lake after running their wolves through the woods. Soap wasn't a requirement and was usually too scented.

Speaking of which, he should check the woods. There were enough shifters in the area, and he suspected many more lived around Twin Forks but didn't often venture into city limits. Patience mentioned a few isolated colonies that no one probably thought about. And she probably needed some space right now.

"I need to go for a run," he said.

"Okay." She continued sorting her trays.

"No. Like, I need to change and run."

"Don't you have sweats?" She jerked her head up. "*Oh*. So, is there anything I should or shouldn't do while you run?"

"Don't look out the window."

"I'm not supposed to see you as a wolf?"

He cocked his head. "Have you ever seen a shifter as a wolf?"

"Yes."

After the encounter with Tamera, he needed a little levity. He let his grin show, nice and slow. "It's not seeing me as a wolf that's an issue. It's that I have to strip every stitch off to do it."

Her cheeks flushed a pretty pink and she straightened, her milk-filled ice trays forgotten. "You need privacy."

"I don't care," he drawled. "We're not a shy species."

"I won't look." Her scent filled his nostrils—the most fragrant bloom of meadow blossoms it'd make Mother Nature jealous.

"Suit yourself." He chuckled as he walked out, but his teasing had backfired. He hoped she didn't look out the window. It was going to be hard enough to shift with another painful erection.

CHAPTER 7

*P*atience glanced at the time. It was the end of her shift, but Kalli hadn't shown up yet for her weekend of work. That was the only plus to this job, and a major reason why Patience didn't go back to school for a counseling degree. Then she'd get stuck with everyone's weekend shift.

It was hard enough to milk Dot regularly as it was.

Only, it hadn't been hard the previous week. She suspected Malcolm liked spoiling the goats with treats after he milked Dot. And then there were the chickens. The roosters never crowed before she woke up anymore and the hens seemed to lay more eggs, just for Malcolm.

He spoiled them, too.

And Tripod and Shaggy. The dogs were shameless, and since their coats were glowing, she thought Malcolm must brush them every day. Spring shedding and clumping hadn't been an issue this year.

The indoor cats were worse. Chip and Dale hadn't slept with her all week. She found them dozing in Malcolm's still-warm and folded blankets on the couch.

She'd relaxed about him learning more about how she'd gone against the laws of his kind. He asked about work when she got home, and by yesterday, his tone sounded more curious than interrogating.

They were comfortable around each other and he was comfortable on her property.

And no one but Jacob, her neighbors, and—*ugh*—Tamera, knew about him.

She finished taking inventory of their pantry. The soap was getting low, but she was making a batch this weekend. There were enough non-perishables to get through Saturday and Sunday.

Four boxes of donated kids' clothing were piled by the door of their giveaway room. Several families fled without much more than a suitcase, if that. New Horizons took donations and added them to their free thrift area.

She hauled the boxes to the thrift room, set them down on a nearby table, and flipped on the light. A mess greeted her.

"Lazy bastards. All of them." She was only an assistant, but her coworkers took their schooling to mean that they didn't have to organize, straighten, or unload donated materials. Neither did they think they had to fill the paper towel dispensers in the bathrooms, or heaven forbid, the toilet paper rolls.

They assumed that she was their assistant in all ways. Including being late for the Friday evening shift.

She scanned the room. Tables full of clothing that had once been neatly arranged were a jumbled mess, boxes of diapers looked like they were used as life-sized building blocks, and the toiletries table looked like it had tipped over and been righted.

Apparently, a family came in last night looking to replenish supplies and the kids went wild, and the evening shift didn't bother to pick up. They knew she was working today.

With a sigh, she started at one table and worked her way around, tidying and sorting stacks back into their sizes and emptying the new boxes while she was at it. She had to throw out half of each box. The people they helped were in a rough spot and didn't deserve soiled and stained clothing and busted toys.

Her phone buzzed. She pulled it out and frowned at the unfamiliar number. "Hello?"

"I thought you'd be home by now," Malcolm's terse voice flowed through the line and stroked her eardrums. Was there one part of her body that didn't crave him?

"My replacement isn't here. Why?"

A beat of silence passed. "I was worried."

The spread of her smile matched the warmth flowing throughout her body. "Oh, in that case, I'm plotting with Jacob about how we're going to keep our big bad secrets away from you."

It was safer to tease over the phone. He couldn't smell her anxiety.

What did she smell like to him, anyway?

She took a discreet sniff of her shirt as he said, "Ha-ha. It's getting dark soon. Shoot me a message before you leave."

"I've been working here since I turned eighteen. How do you think I survived without you?"

"Luck."

She sputtered out a laugh. "That's me. Miss Lucky. I actually had a cat named that once. She was missing an eye and three toes when I found her."

"How many cats have you—never mind. Just shoot me a message, okay?"

"Okay, *Dad*." She really did appreciate his concern, but couldn't resist.

"Not funny," he growled.

A beep cut him off. She looked at the screen. "Oh, hey. That's Kalli calling. I gotta go." She didn't wait for his acceptance, but clicked over. "Hey, Kalli."

"Patience, I'm so sorry. Gretchen is sick and Todd has the swing shift." Patience rolled her eyes. Kallie's husband always has the swing shift—it was like his schedule magically synched up with hers so Kalli could justify why she couldn't work. "Can you take tonight?"

And tomorrow, she'd probably call because Gretchen would still be sick and there'd be another reason she couldn't take her weekend shift. "I actually have company."

"Oh, she's throwing up. Sorry, Patience, I have to go." Kalli hung up.

Patience glowered at her phone. The first few times Kalli did this after having Gretchen, she hadn't thought anything of it. She wanted to help her coworker out. Working when you had kids was tough.

But it'd been years of dropped shifts, and other coworkers seem to use Kalli as a role model for how not to look for another replacement or plan for vacations and to drop their shifts on Patience.

She went into the main office and left a note on Jacob's desk. She never talked to him about how often shifts were dumped on her and he never asked. It wasn't a job that was easy to find a replacement for and since he carried a lot of stress as the boss, she didn't add more to his plate.

But it got tiresome.

And she had a sexy shifter at home.

She had no idea how long Malcolm would stay. She also had no clue what he was doing as far as investigating her. He seemed content to hang out at her place and spoil her animals.

Why had he been on a hiatus from his job? He was a mess

when she found him, but nothing about what he'd done in the last week suggested he was going through some issues.

She left the note on Jacob's keyboard. As she was leaving, her phone rang again.

This time it was Jacob. She answered. "I was just leaving you a note. Kalli called in. Sick kid."

"That's too bad. You're at work then?" He sounded more relieved than sympathetic.

"Yes."

"Oh good. I wasn't sure how I could talk to you with, you know, your...visitor." Jacob had been checking in with her throughout the week, concerned about her safety, but she'd updated him each day at work since she forbid him from coming to her place. Malcolm was being patient, but she wanted to keep Jacob from him as long as possible.

Or, she wanted to keep *him* as long as possible.

"So, about Dad," Jacob continued. "He said thanks for the heads up. He and Millie will stay away from Twin Forks."

Good. But really, it's not like they ever came around. "Thank you for getting them the message."

"No problem. Well, I'll let you go," Jacob said. "Thanks for filling in for Kalli."

"Did I have any choice?"

"Hmm? What was that?"

Was it a case of selective hearing, or had he really not heard her? Someday, she'd have to talk to him.

Then they'd both feel like crap and Kalli might quit and find another job. Since Jocelyn and Nalini were also counselors, they might choose to move to a town with higher pay than take more hours. There could be a mass exodus. Then she and Jacob would both be stuck working too much.

She'd been looking forward to a Friday night with Malcolm. He always came in after his nightly runs and dropped on the chair by the couch and watched what she was watching on TV. She looked forward to it.

Right. Malcolm.

She punched out a quick text to him to let him know she'd be staying until eleven when Jocelyn came in.

The next hour went by quickly as she finished straightening the thrift room. Her stomach started to rumble. She'd only packed enough for lunch and the break room fridge probably had mold growing in every container. She held off cleaning the fridge, but since it was quiet, she might put it on her to-do list.

She went through the pantry that clients got to use. She'd replace whatever she took before she worked her next shift.

Looking through the shelves, she had chicken noodle soup, Spaghetti-Os, and canned ravioli to choose from. She made her own chicken soup, but she could swing by the store and grab a few cans to replace what she took.

A soft thunk made her jump and spin around. The doors were locked, they had a bell for clients. No one should be in here.

"Kalli?" Was it possible she made it to work after all?

She hefted a soup can and edged out, peering down the hallway. A wick of cool air ruffled her hair. Her heart squeezed.

She wasn't alone.

"How the hell are you planning to defend yourself with that?"

She shrieked and jumped, spinning toward the voice and chucking the can. By the time it left her fingers, she'd registered the voice as Malcolm's.

He snatched the soup out of the air, a slight smile dancing over his lips.

"How'd you get in?" she screeched. The employee

entrance required a key card and the front entrance was locked. They had a doorbell that he obviously didn't use.

"You think a human lock can stop me?" He tossed the can of soup between his hands. "What else do you have to defend yourself with if someone attacks?"

"No one's broken into the center the entire time it's been open."

He rolled his eyes, ratcheting up her irritation. How dare he sneak in and give her a heart attack? Now if something did happen in the future, she was going to secretly hope it was a sexy shifter when it might be an enraged spouse.

"And how long has that been?" he asked.

"New Horizons has been open for forty years. My mom started the place." She looked around, not bothering to hide her pride.

His brows lifted. "Really?" He hefted a backpack she hadn't noticed in her fright. "I figured you didn't pack anything for dinner, and since I have yet to come here, I thought now would be a good time."

Her tiny flicker of hope died inside. He brought her some food, but lest she think someone like him would see her as more than his job, he did it as an excuse to check out the place. But he was right. No one else was here and they wouldn't have to justify his presence.

She folded her arms and smothered her hurt. "If a client comes, you'll have to hide. Most of who we help are women running from men. It wouldn't do to have them see you as soon as they step inside."

Him, with his brawny build and rough-around-the-edges beard.

"They'd never know I'm here."

She eyed the backpack. "Did you eat already?"

"No. I packed sandwiches, but they might be a bit

jumbled. I had to carry the bag in my mouth on the way here."

She cocked her head, trying to picture him driving with a bag in his mouth.

"I ran here," he explained.

"You were naked, in town?"

"No one saw."

They didn't know what they were missing. Neither did she, and that was for the best.

"I figured I could catch a ride with you," he continued.

"I work until eleven."

"Yep." He wandered down the hall, checking each door, probably looking for a break room. "That gives you *hours* to tell me what you do here."

MALCOLM PROWLED THE YARD. Last night at New Horizons had been enlightening, just not in the way he'd hoped. Yet, he couldn't regret spending an evening getting the grand tour and long explanations from Patience. He'd stayed until the end of her shift. And it made him restless today. He had no more answers than before.

HE'D ALREADY RUN through the woods, sniffing around for new scents, keeping a keen nose out for anything that spelled trouble. Patience's part of the world was the last one that'd make him think something sinister would happen, but he wasn't letting his guard down.

Bad people happened everywhere.

There was a mystery to solve in Twin Forks, and he had little idea what it involved. Like why a small, secluded community teeming with humans attracted so many shifters, and why they tolerated Patience and Jacob knowing about them. Shifters were inherently distrustful of humans, but he could see why having a few connections would help.

Would it justify her and her brother keeping their memories?

It was getting harder for him not to search for reasons to let her do just that, to justify her knowledge to his commander and the Synod.

His brother's mate, Sylva, would have a serious soft spot for Patience. Working at a women's shelter earned automatic respect from his new sister. She'd come from an atrocious relationship and rose to the top of their government, but that didn't mean she still didn't carry those scars.

Scars that his twin soothed as often as he could.

Envy gnawed at Malcolm. He had a place with his twin and Sylva at her cottage hours north of Twin Forks, just past the Canadian border, but staying there made him pace like a tiger at the zoo. Back and forth, back and forth, restlessness and too many questions eating away at him.

Could Camille have made it this far—if she survived whatever happened to her?

His home town of Tame Peaks was a few hours east and north. It wasn't an easy place to get to on paved roads. A wolf would have more freedom, but there were still a couple hundred miles to travel on foot, through human and mountain lion territory. Shifters were big and strong and healed from most things, but they also didn't want to ask for unnecessary fights.

Would she have come here willingly? He tried to calculate the years. As young as he was, the years blended together. If he'd gone to high school like a normal human, he'd have been just past nineteen when Camille disappeared.

His phone buzzed and he winced inwardly. Dot gazed at

him from across the yard. He pulled it out of his pocket and frowned when he saw the caller.

As if thinking about his sister summoned Maw... "Everything all right?" he answered.

"Why the fuck wouldn't it be?" Maw responded, her gravelly voice both familiar and so painfully foreign at the same time. He hadn't seen her much since he'd left home. Short messages that likely ended in her throwing the phone across the house, pissed off at the tiny screen. Maw was a female of action, never sitting still, but she was still a mother and surprised him with a flash of caring once in a while.

"Because you're actually calling."

"Can't a mother do that?"

Sure. But not her. "How you doing, Maw?"

"Not human, so that's better than anything."

He dropped to the top step of Patience's porch. Maw and her hatred of humans. "Hear from Father?"

She snorted. "He's living the dream. Gets waited on hand and foot and doesn't have to be responsible for no one."

That sounded right. Each of his parents came with a load of baggage and had packed a few more bags in their time together. Malcolm wondered how they were physically together long enough to procreate. "Harrison said he stops in once in a while."

"That's my boy. Always a good kid." Maternal pride rang in her voice, but it was mostly from Harrison nailing Sylva as a mate. Another family member at the top of their species. "What are you up to?"

"I'm in Twin Forks, working."

"That doesn't sound like a shifter town."

"It's not, really." But it was more of a shifter town than anyone thought.

Maw wasn't a traditional nurturing maternal figure. She could make a mean strawberry-rhubarb pie, but she also cussed out her sons and anyone around and kept to herself. Losing Camille had been hard and she'd depended on him and Harrison to find her and bring her home. Sometimes, he wondered if their failure was the reason he and his twin stayed away from both Maw and Father.

Maybe that's what propelled him to tell Maw what he was up to. She sensed something was off with him and called. He owed it to her to tell her. "I took some time off. Camille—"

"You ain't gonna find her, Malcolm." Maw sounded resigned to the fate of never knowing what happened. It was his fault he never found out for her.

"I have to try."

Her reply was silence at first. He was used to awkward conversations with Maw. They didn't happen often, but when they did, they were halting and weird. Like, she didn't know what to do or say and would rather prattle on, swearing about how stupid the pack was that currently ran his little hometown.

"Go ahead and try," she finally said. "But it ain't gonna bring her back."

"Do you know anything about what happened that day?" Other than Camille leaving to take her horse on the trails she'd carved through the woods, they had no leads. She and the horse had vanished. Without a trace.

"I know that if she's not dead, she's not coming back." It was the same thing Maw said every time. *If she ain't dead, she ain't coming back.* He never understood why his cantankerous Maw couldn't let go of how Solange Gibson next door dared put a fence one inch over the property line, but she was all *there's nothing we can do* when it came to Camille.

"I have to try, Maw," he said quietly, beseeching her to understand. Harrison got it, but he'd let Camille go. Since he was middle-aged in human years, his boss treated him like he was having a midlife crisis.

Hell, maybe he was. He'd been killing more than a week on a hobby farm, feeding goats and feeling better than he had in a while.

Along with hornier, but that was something he tried not to think about on an ordinary day, and definitely not on the phone with his Maw. If she ever thought he had his eye on a human, she'd go nuclear.

Maw blew out a gusty sigh, which was probably billowing with smoke. Not many shifters could tolerate that many chemicals infiltrating their bodies, but Maw grew the tobacco and dried and hand-rolled her own.

Gave her something to do other than yelling over the fence at Solange.

"Go ahead and try, but just think, Malcolm. If she didn't die, and you find her after all these years, what are you going to do?"

"Do you think she's really alive?" That wasn't the part Maw wanted him to hang onto, but he did.

"She's my girl. She was stubborn and lived to disobey, but she was mine. If anyone's a survivor, it would be her." There was a pregnant pause. "But that doesn't mean that she did."

"I understand. I just want answers."

"Be careful. You just might get them. Ah, shit. What the hell is that bitch doing now? I've gotta go, but hey, be careful and don't fuck around with humans." Maw hung up without saying goodbye, the sound of a leaf blower cutting off with it.

Some things never changed and if they did, he'd miss it. Humans disgusted Maw, and if any shifter ever mated one, she loudly disowned them. It didn't matter if she hardly talked to them in the first place.

Don't fuck around with humans.

What the hell was he doing here?

Staring at the phone in his hands, he willed himself to call and check in with his commander. He didn't have much to report, and he didn't have much reason for not having made more progress.

He could spin it as a delicate situation. He was surrounded by humans and couldn't go charging in to ask questions. But he hadn't even met Jacob yet.

The tour Patience gave him last night, how proud she was of the center and how much of her he noticed in the environment, that place meant a lot to her. The subtle, soft scents of her soaps permeated the hallways. She organized the pantry and the thrift room like she did her own house. Tidy, but not obsessive.

The watercolors on the wall were her dad's she'd said, and she also mentioned that he was gone. He didn't ask more beyond inquiring how long ago she'd lost her parents.

I didn't know him well. Mom died when I was a baby and I lost Dad before I was potty trained.

He had both parents and hardly talked with them. She had no one but her brother, a guy who was okay with her working double shifts and the occasional twenty-four.

He'd asked how often that happened, but she'd brushed him off. So, a lot.

His pretty little human. A powerhouse in the most unassuming package. He grew more fascinated with her the longer he was here.

Not good.

He made the call.

"Have something for me?" the commander answered.

"Not much. I'm taking it slow. Humans." He grimaced at his weak as hell explanation.

"Treading carefully isn't a bad idea." His commander's even tone was hard to read.

"She's a stable person. Runs a hobby farm and works overtime at a women's shelter. I haven't met her brother yet, but I want to take that slow, come up with a good story."

"Where are you staying?"

"With…her."

He cringed at the commander's initial silence. "I don't have to remind you that wiping her mind will be harder if you're attached to her."

"I know what's involved, and I'm not involved with her."

"Not at all?" The disbelief was easy to read.

"She didn't jump me, no. And I'm not using her. She's… she's a good person."

More silence. "Maybe you should find a hotel."

"Then my presence would bring up more questions. Right now, if we run across shifters, they'll just think she's a temporary plaything." He bristled at the thought. Patience with her wide blue eyes and straight forward stare wasn't temporary. She was the real deal.

"And she's not."

"Not what?" The image of Patience's ass swaying as she walked to the barn with the milk pail distracted him.

"A plaything."

"No," he growled.

"I see. Listen, I'm going to update Harrison—"

"I can do it."

"—and tell him to be ready to go at a moment's notice."

"Commander—"

"Malcolm. You're going through some shit and sleeping over with some single woman who raises goats and rescues dogs might not be the best thing for you."

Everything the commander said was true. Didn't make it right, or right for him. He couldn't leave. Walking away would be like trudging through mud with concrete boots.

And no one else, not even his brother, was touching Patience's pretty little head.

"Give me more time, Commander."

"I'm giving you time, but I also want backup ready to go. Harrison could get there in a few hours."

"Fine," he bit out. "But I'm doing my job." However slowly.

"I'm not saying you aren't. But some jobs become more personal than others, and you already have personal issues." The edge was honed off his voice enough that Malcolm listened.

"Thank you, sir."

He hung up and shoved his hand through his hair.

What the hell was he doing?

A furry orange tabby swiped against him. Without thinking, he hauled the cat into his lap and scratched behind his ears. It'd become their after-run ritual. The tabby would wait by the stairs for his scritches, and Malcolm was more than happy to obey.

And when he sat like this, he could pretend there were no personal issues and that there was no chance of hurting Patience when this was all over.

CHAPTER 8

*M*alcolm had been gone much of the previous day. When he came back, Patience had supper ready and he ate his portion and what would normally be her leftovers for the week.

Good thing she didn't rely on Dot for her own milk supply. She couldn't stomach goat milk and Dot would be drained dry while Malcolm was here.

But she had enough food that she shouldn't have to get groceries until after work tomorrow. She tried not to go to town on her days off, and the last foray with Damian hadn't turned out well. That didn't mean it wasn't informative.

Now that she'd gotten over the shock of Malcolm and Tamera, she'd had time to process the short conversation between them.

He couldn't perform?

The day she found him, he'd said the shifters at the bar assumed the worst of him and attacked. And that he was here on personal business. But he was shell-shocked to see Tamera, so she wasn't his personal business.

What was his story?

Pondering everything related to Malcolm helped keep the seething jealousy at bay. She didn't like Tamera. She dreaded crossing her, dreaded being in her line of sight. The last thing she needed was to be jealous. She'd never had a reason before. Sure, the female was gorgeous, but she was also another species, one that Patience could never compete with.

Yet, she didn't think Malcolm was wound up over the female shifter. Stunned. Confused. But not pining for her. He'd been hurt terribly, and those effects continued to linger inside of him.

And it all meant that Patience had less of a chance with him than ever, in the event hell would freeze over and what she'd been doing with her brother helping shifters wasn't illegal in Malcolm's world, that is.

So, no. No reason to be jealous.

He was gone again, out for a run. She finished her soap and was in the basement arranging the molds. The dogs' barking grabbed her attention first. Was there a visitor, or had a jackrabbit streaked through her yard?

The house shuddered under the front door slam. A tremor coursed down her spine.

"It's just Malcolm," she muttered to herself. But something about the way the door slammed was very unlike the large bearded male that'd been her guest for a few days now.

He never slammed the door.

And her dogs never barked at him. Not even when he shifted. They only whined because they couldn't keep up with him and had to slink back home before they became mountain lion bait.

She crept out of the pantry-turned-soap-curing room. There was a shotgun in the tiny entry closet upstairs, but if her visitor wasn't Malcolm, then he was closer to the shotgun than her.

Grandma kept an old pistol down here. Patience had left

it, just in case, but had never needed to use it. Was it even loaded?

"I know you're home, bitch," a male voice snarled. "Get out here."

Her heart crammed into her throat. Had Damian woken up and remembered everything?

It didn't sound like him, but the male sounded enraged.

"Get the fuck out here and tell me where she is."

Oh, *shit*. It'd always been a possibility that the angry spouse of one of the women she helped would find her. Everyone in town knew who she and Jacob were and what they did, but there were so many surrounding small towns and Twin Forks had amenities the others didn't. Plenty of strangers streaming in and out of town. Patience made it a habit to watch her surroundings and have an escape plan, but after more than a decade of doing the job, she'd grown complacent. Her gaze swept the basement. There was furniture from nearly fifty years ago down here, the set from before Grandma had last updated. The couch was big enough for her to hide behind.

Heavy footsteps stomped through the house. Dust filtered down from the drop ceiling tiles. She turned off all the lights she could reach and scurried to the couch.

Where had she left the pistol again? She never had kids over. Why hadn't she left it out and ready somewhere?

Because she never thought she'd be cornered in the basement she hardly spent any time in.

The footsteps grew more muted. Whoever it was, was probably tossing her bedroom. What if he did worse? She was stuck in a basement with a house so old that Grandma never worried about safety when it came to the narrow rectangular windows. There were no egress dig-outs to accommodate windows a person could escape through. It wasn't until now that she realized the basement was nothing but a large coffin in the case of a fire—or an angry intruder who'd probably kill her. Because there was no way she was giving up the location of any of the people she helped.

She dove behind the couch, its feet scraping the worn orange carpeting as it shifted away from the wall.

Dammit. She should've crawled in backward. She faced the far corner of the basement, the stairs behind her. Her intruder would check the basement next. She'd left the door hanging open when she'd brought the soap molds down. As soon as he entered the kitchen, he'd figure out where she was.

Think, Patience.

He hadn't located her yet. Could she safely assume that it was a man and not a shifter? Did that make it any better?

He hadn't fired any shots so he may not have a gun on him. A knife? Was he strong enough to tear her apart?

She had a better chance of fighting a human male. And since he'd found her house, she had to assume that the "her" he was looking for lived in the area. A couple that lived in or near Twin Forks?

That didn't help her, but maybe she'd be able to talk to him.

"Found you, you bitch."

She flinched and craned her head to look behind her. He hadn't found her. The light over the basement stairs was on and he only assumed she was down here.

He was right, but maybe he'd do a sweep and not find her and she'd luck out.

Luck hadn't been the most abundant lately.

Footsteps pounded down the stairs and he kicked in the door to the storage room, what used to be the old laundry room before she and Jacob had moved in.

"I'm gonna find you. Might as well come out. All I wanna do is talk." His restrained voice said that talking wasn't all that'd happen. "You took my wife away. My kids. The least you could do is *face me*."

Her breathing was ragged in her ears and she tried to keep it down.

A familiar scratching sound caught her attention. What was that?

"Maybe I'll just burn the whole place down."

A lighter. She wasn't a smoker, but sometimes the clients did, and since they were going through a traumatic time, they often chain-smoked while they were at the center. And flicked their lighter nervously like this man was doing.

"How 'bout I start with this cushion?" His footsteps whispered closer.

She bit her cheek until she tasted blood, willing to call his bluff. Praying it *was* a bluff.

His steps maneuvered away. "Maybe I start the fire upstairs. Smoke you out—if you're lucky enough to fit out them damn windows."

She'd make herself fit.

He whipped the couch away from her. It crashed into the end table and bounced back on its four feet.

"Found you," he sneered.

She scooted out of his reach, but his meaty hand clamped harder than a vise around her bicep and dragged her over the carpet. She dug her fingers in, but to no avail. Kicking out, she twisted but he cocked his arm. She barely had time to throw her other arm over her face before he struck.

A punishing blow bounced off her forearm. She yelped but continued to struggle.

"Where is she?"

It didn't matter who he was asking about, Patience would never tell. Ever. He could torture and kill her, but she dedicated her life to helping others. She wasn't going back on all her work. Besides, if she did tell him, he might just kill her and be done with it.

She kept twisting and writhing. He tried to beat her into submission. Blows glanced off her shoulder and her arms. Protecting herself as much as she could, she anchored her feet on the wall and shoved.

It unbalanced him, and his grip on her slipped. She did it again, using her whole body to plow into him. He stumbled back and the off-kilter couch caught his legs. He fell back. And she ran.

Her phone was on the kitchen counter. If she could get upstairs, grab it on her way out, she could call 911 as she fled.

She sprinted for the stairs, swinging the perpetually open door at the base of the steps closed behind her.

"You bitch!"

The door didn't latch, but hearing it rip open and rebound off the wall from the force told her that he was right behind her. She took the stairs as fast as she could. Her skin crawled, awareness prickling over her until she wanted to crawl out of her body. A loud thump sounded close behind her.

She risked a glance. He'd dived for her feet and missed. It gave her an extra second.

The phone was right where she left it. Snagging it as she raced by, she ran for the front door.

Banging out the screen door, she prepared to put on as much speed as she could but ran into a wall.

Strong arms closed around her.

A strangled scream tore out of her and she looked up, afraid of who she'd find. Had he not come alone?

A furious—and very naked—Malcolm glared over her head, his eyes narrowed. He set her aside like she was one of her grandma's dolls. She winced at the pain, and he jerked his gaze back to her.

"Did he hurt you?"

She only managed a nod and backed up. The cold rage in Malcolm's eyes was nothing like the crazed fury in the intruder's.

Malcolm opened the screen door so hard it ripped one hinge out of the jamb. The man sped around the corner and skidded to a stop.

"What the fuck?" The man's gaze raked over Malcolm, derision darkening his gaze. His mouth was bleeding. Patience didn't know if she'd landed any punches or if he face-planted on the stairs. "Who the hell are you?"

Malcolm didn't answer. He reached out, fisted his hand around the man's collar and yanked him out of the house, throwing him off the porch in one move. The man bounced and rolled, his moan swallowed up by the silence of the yard.

Her animals were uncharacteristically quiet as they watched the scene.

Malcolm stalked down the stairs of her porch. Tripod and Shaggy circled the other side of her assailant, like they decided to form a small pack with only her and Malcolm and this person was not invited.

Malcolm leaned over him, jerked on his collar again, and brought the man nose-to-nose. "Who. The fuck. Are you?"

"That bitch—"

Malcolm shoved him so hard his head bounced off the ground. Patience jumped, her hand clenching around the phone in her hand. She had to call the police, but she was mesmerized by the calm force that was Malcolm.

"Call her that again and I'll toss you across the yard, and I'll keep doing it until your body is nothing but a skin bag over bone shards." Menace oozed from Malcolm, but like the animals, she wasn't scared for herself.

She had enough sense to be scared for the human and the outcome of any overt force Malcolm might use.

"Malcolm. I need to call the police."

He pinned her under his direct stare. The man tried to wiggle away, his hands and legs futilely scrabbling against the grass, but Malcolm's hold was ironclad. "He hurt you."

"But he's…" She glanced from the intruder to Malcolm and mouthed *human*.

"Fine."

She made the call. Malcolm stayed poised and the man didn't try to escape.

An engine roared down her drive. Was there a deputy that close to her place?

It was Brenden. Delia sat next to him, and they had a passenger.

Fucking Tamera. As if getting physically attacked wasn't enough, she had to deal with verbal abuse.

WITH BRENDEN AND DELIA THERE, Malcolm ran back to his clothing and changed. When he turned around, Tamera was right there.

"What the hell are you doing here?" He sighed as he said it. His adrenaline had been riding high until he turned around.

He was dealing with human police. The last thing he needed was her scrambling his brains.

"I'm staying with Brenden and Delia for a while."

His ears pricked at the sirens in the distance. The cops would be here soon. "I've got to go."

"They have it under control." She crept closer. She'd probably watched him get dressed, which was nothing for his kind, but seemed rude on Patience's property. "Besides, it's better if Brenden claims he was the one who helped Patience out. It'd be harder to explain you."

Dammit. She had a good point. Brenden's facial hair was more of a dark shadow, but it wasn't like the authorities would believe a man who'd attack a lone woman in the middle of nowhere and not her presumably sedate neighbor.

"I need to get closer." He had to hear what they were saying.

She put her hand on his chest. Memories drifted up. How they'd lie next to each other and stare at the stars, murmuring about what they were going to do when they were older. He'd talk about being a Guardian and helping his kind like his father did—this was before he realized how corrupt their former government was, and how his father didn't use his position to put a stop to it.

Tamera would talk about... He frowned. He couldn't remember. Surely, she'd had dreams and passions she spoke of, but usually, they ended up having sex.

And she'd never allowed him to officially claim her and give her his bite during orgasm. It'd let everyone know she was his.

We're too young, she'd said. *We have plenty of time.*

But she never planned to be with him.

"I need to let Patience know I'm still here," he said gruffly.

"I told them I'd come tell you about the plan. Deputy Barnes doesn't have to know you or I were ever here." She swayed closer, her pelvis touching his. He backed up a step, and she let her hand fall. Frowning, she asked, "Why are you in Twin Forks in the first place? You never really answered."

He hadn't been able to answer it himself. He wavered between telling her and not. That initial pull to talk to her like he used to was still there, but it was muted. She'd broken what they had. Did he want it back?

That was the problem. He felt like he should, but... wouldn't those feelings be stronger?

"Camille," he said. Tamera had stayed until he and Harrison left on their yearlong search for Camille. Then she'd left him. He always wondered if that year away only showed her how much better life was without him.

Something flickered in Tamera's eyes, but he couldn't identify it. "You found her?"

He shook his head, his throat growing thick, making it hard for words to come out. "No, but the last mission I was on made me think of her. Her disappearance... It's gnawing at me. I need to know what happened."

"Oh, Mal." She sighed and tilted her head back to stare through the canopy of trees over their heads. "Always the good boy. The dutiful one."

"You make it sound like a bad thing."

Her expression filled with sadness. "It isn't, if those duties work for you. But if they imprison you, well..."

"You felt trapped?"

"I didn't feel trapped," she said tightly. "I *was* trapped."

"I don't understand. If we mated, we would've left. We would've lived by Freemont and West Creek." He used to think about what might have been with regret and longing, but this time, he said it as more of an observation. A way to understand how she'd felt.

"You and I both know your Maw would've wanted you back. Either you or Harrison had to follow in your father's footsteps, and no one liked Harrison enough."

His brother was the dark and brooding one. Their good cop/bad cop routine had worked several times over the decades. "So you mated someone else to keep from living in Tame Peaks?"

"Darius was a live-and-let-live kind of male. It was the

only way I could leave Tame Peaks and live on my own terms."

"Mated. To someone else." Did they grow up with different ideas of mating?

"You wouldn't have tolerated half the shit Darius didn't care about. He was centuries old, hadn't found his own mate, and was worried about going feral. I knew we were compatible."

Malcolm wondered if that was his future. He was young in shifter years, but there wasn't a set date that a lonely bastard lost his or her mind without a mate. Since he'd had a mate and she chose another, he didn't think lightning would strike twice on his heart.

And he couldn't change the past. He held a grudge against Darius, but not enough to wish bad things on him. "I'm sorry about what happened to him."

Her smile was sad. "He went the way he wanted to go. Living life to the fullest. Because of him, three human fire-fighters are still around. They're planning a memorial to Darius in front of the fire department. He would've gotten a kick out of the irony."

Shifters and fire weren't often compatible, and Darius would be memorialized. He almost chuckled at the irony she mentioned. And it hit him. He had no more hard feelings toward the late shifter.

All of that was gone. Off his shoulders. In its place was confusion.

What now? Tamera was here, but that old feeling between them? He couldn't detect it. What did that mean? Were they supposed to be together or did Tamera get the independence she wanted while he got a life sentence of insanity?

He couldn't think here, next to her. She brought the swirling, suffocating emotions from his past to this peaceful farm that Patience ran.

Peaceful, except for the human who almost murdered her. If he hadn't been on his way back from his run...

Tamera tilted her head, inspecting him. "You're upset. You weren't before."

"I want that human taken care of."

Her expression hardened. "Don't worry. Rescue Rabbit is fine. You swooped in and saved her."

"Why do you call her that?"

"Does it bother you?"

He answered honestly. "Only because it bothers her."

Calculating interest infused her amber irises. "And you're concerned about a human? What would your mother say?"

She'd pin him with that steely glare and suck her teeth until he stammered out an explanation. "Human or not, she's a good person."

"Mmm. Too good, I'm sure you'll find out." He was about to ask what she meant when she rushed on. "She rescues all sorts of animals. My neighbor has a fucking squirrel Patience nursed to health when she found it as a baby, abandoned and injured. A squirrel. They're snacks, not pets. And she's a timid human, never stands up for herself. Those big eyes. That twitching nose. Her round ass. She's like a bunny. Rescue Rabbit."

"Quit being a bitch to her, Tam."

Her expression cooled. "You never used to mind my nicknames before."

Probably because they were shifters. If a shifter couldn't deal with an unwanted nickname themselves, it was more than a matter of pride. It could be a dangerous sign of weakness. He also hadn't been around his Maw for a few decades and wasn't used to that behavior on a daily basis. Even for shifters, it was toxic.

Patience wasn't a shifter, and he didn't want anything toxic around her.

"I guess we've both changed."

Tamera arched a light brow, her expression haughty. "We might have, but if Patience doesn't like what I say, she can damn well take care of it herself." Her voice dropped low. "And you and I both know damn well that she isn't strong enough to."

She stomped away, branches and dried grass from the previous fall crunching under her feet.

He shook his head and let her go on without him. She was circling behind the house, presumably going back to Delia and Brenden's. He hadn't heard the cop car leaving so he squatted down between a couple of firs where he couldn't be seen by the human eye and waited.

After several more minutes, a car pulled away. He crept through the tree line and around the barn. Dot and Betsy loped to the edge of their pen. He reached over and scratched each one on the head.

Patience stood next to Delia and Brenden, wearing the black leggings and baggy T-shirt she made soap in, her arms wrapped around herself. Her words drifted on the tepid breeze to his ears. "No, really. I'm fine. Thanks for the offer, but I'll be okay."

Delia's brows pinched and her gaze touched on him. He read the decision in her eyes. As long as he was here, she and Brenden would go. "All right, then. But call if you need anything."

"Thanks for rushing over when you heard…"

"I'm glad I was outside to hear it." Brenden lifted his chin toward him. "And that Malcolm got here when he did."

To think the crash that had drawn him to the house was Patience being beaten made his canines throb. He didn't pay that fucker back enough.

"I'd better get inside. Thank you." Her gaze touched on him and jumped away. "All of you." She shuffled back to the house, missing the usual spring in her step. That alone stoked his rage.

"What was the story?" Malcolm asked, his gaze not leaving Patience.

"Last week," Delia answered, "a woman took her kids and left that bastard—for a damn good reason. Travis is his name. He thought Patience was an easy target."

"He thought wrong," Malcolm growled. He looked at Brenden. "Thanks again."

"It was easy to fool the deputy. The bastard argued, but the deputy didn't give a shit."

Good. His gut wanted him to go after Patience. No matter what she said, she wasn't all right. He tipped his head toward the house. "I'd better go check on her."

"Just doing your job?" Brenden asked lightly, but his question was loaded.

"Like I told Tam, human or not, there's no reason to be a dick."

"You told Tamera that?" Delia asked. "About Patience?"

"Yeah." He'd ask why it was a big deal, but this conversation was taking too long as it was. He jogged to the house, ignoring them.

The screen was hanging off. Patience must've stepped around it rather than dealing with it, or she was trying to find her tools.

He hadn't seen the damage inside the house yet. The entry and main levels weren't bad. Travis had shoved furniture aside during his hunt. Malcolm could trace his path by that alone.

He followed the scent of meadow blossoms to his right, through the kitchen and downstairs. Shuffling and faint scrapes came from the stairs to the basement. She'd been down there when the intruder found her. The furniture was scattered and pushed closer to one wall.

He took the stairs lightly. He didn't want to scare her, but she didn't need to hear another set of heavy footfalls on the stairs. He'd been around enough domestic fights to know how it all played out.

Patience came into sight. The delicate smell of all her curing soap filled the basement, but it was a comfort, like she knew the right amount to not offend his shifter senses. She was trying to muscle a big, floral-patterned couch back to its feet. There were fresh shoe marks on the wall and a few dents around them. She'd been hiding behind the couch when he found her.

"Let me help."

She yelped and jumped, her hand covered her heart. Then her face flushed, and shame infiltrated her scent. Her gaze darted away before she turned her back on him.

Flinging her arm out, she gestured around. "It's, um, not as bad as it looks. I thought…I thought…it'd be worse."

"Hey, Patience." He tenderly touched her shoulder and she flinched.

"Oh, wow. That hurts already. I guess he hit me more than I thought."

She tried to play nonchalant, but her normally tranquil scent pinged all over the place.

He kept his touch deliberately light and turned her around. Her eyes were watery and she couldn't look at him.

"It's okay to be scared," he murmured, brushing a tear that escaped to course down her cheek. He cupped her face. She was going to have a few small bruises across her cheeks and chin, but that likely meant the rest of her body took the brunt of it. She'd admirably defended herself against a larger attacker and even managed to outrun him.

"You and-and the others, you all were so calm and-and…I do this for a living and—"

"You don't get the shit beaten out of you for a living. You help others escape what you just went through."

She squeezed her eyes together and he pulled her in, wrapping his arms around her. What she had on this farm, in a few short days, had become his safe space. She was born and raised here, this had been her safe space her entire life. Some asshole ruined that.

Her shoulders shook. She sobbed, her hands twisting into his T-shirt.

He sensed her fatigue. Freeing one arm only to right the sofa, he carefully picked her up and circled it. Lowering them both to the cushions, he arranged her so she laid on top, curled up on his chest.

Those big eyes. That twitching nose. Her round ass. She's like a bunny. Tamera called her that because rabbits were a wolf's natural prey. But there was nothing he wouldn't do to protect Patience.

CHAPTER 9

*P*atience had never been warmer. Odd, in this drafty house, this time of year.

She readjusted on her hard bed.

Wait. This wasn't a bed.

Her eyelids fluttered open and she looked up. Malcolm's steady gaze stared back.

"Feel better?"

Oh God. She'd cried all over him. Bawled like a baby and then fell into a deep sleep. She didn't do that with men, with anyone.

No, she had to hold her shit together all day at work, no matter what stories she heard from the people she helped. She was the steady one, not prone to dramatics.

Forgettable, except to a stalker like Damian who now had forgotten her. Because of the male she was sprawled over.

"You're really warm." She tried to sit up, but his arms were clamped around her.

Okay, they weren't clamped, but he didn't move or act like this was awkward and embarrassing at all.

Her body ached. Bruises were probably forming across

her torso and limbs, but Malcolm was better than any hot pad. The drugging effect of his body against hers made it impossible to leave.

He smiled. His beard looked soft. And so close.

She trailed her hand along it. Malcolm went still, his pupils dilated and his gaze zeroed on her. He was a predator, but she was only emboldened by his reaction.

She shifted until she was on her belly. He let her.

Next, she brushed her fingers along his cheek, up to his hairline, and back down. Was there a world, a universe, an alternate reality where they could be a thing? Even for a little while? Big, fierce male with a heart of gold goes for mousy, soap-making farm girl. "Malcolm?"

"Yeah," he said gruffly.

She couldn't think of what she wanted to say, so she showed him. Wiggling high enough, she didn't miss the long, hard length under her hips. It wasn't his hipbone like she'd thought earlier. It was centered on his body, and the size of it made her insides melt.

Dropping her mouth to his, she just wanted to know what kissing him felt like before he put a stop to it.

But he didn't stop her. She pressed harder, and he met her with equal force. He swept his tongue against her lips and she opened for him.

Shamelessly, she straddled him to get better purchase with his mouth—and to put her throbbing core over that beast of an erection.

Her adrenaline might've crashed after the cops left, but Malcolm woke up her hormones. After so many failed dates and hopeful attempts to meet *the one*, she had someone who might not disappoint her in bed.

His big hands crushed her ass, massaging and kneading. It was the one place on her that probably avoided getting hit.

A moan escaped and she shifted her position, turning her

head to kiss him deeper. She was on top, but he devoured her, kissing her so thoroughly she thought she could come like this.

Then he adjusted her. Rolling up slightly so the arm of the couch was behind his shoulders. He cradled her against him and broke the kiss.

"You need more, don't you, bunny?"

She bit her lip. Getting called Rescue Rabbit was degrading because of the tone. The hot, honeyed way Malcolm said bunny could only make her roll over and bare her everything for him.

"Yes," she whimpered, grinding into him.

"I can give you more."

She lifted her hips the same time that he skimmed his hand around her belly. What was it about him that made her so alive, so wanton, so uncaring of anything else around them?

He captured her mouth again, and she twined her arms around his neck. Tunneling his fingers down her stomach should have filled her with insecurities. How did she look? How bad was her stomach pooching? Should she have taken a shower first?

But he wasn't acting like he cared, so she wouldn't either. When he breached the waistband of her leggings, she squirmed, angling her hips up and allowing him more access.

He took his time, like he savored it. This was a new experience, one straight from her fantasies. Usually, there were bumbling attempts, and every once in a while she'd get off with a partner the few times she found someone willing to take their time to see to her gratification.

But with Malcolm, she was ready to blow as soon as the calloused tip of his finger skated over her clit.

She would've jumped off the couch, but his other arm was banded tightly around her. She sunk into his kiss but anchored her hands on his shoulders. The wicked way he played with her had her both coiled tighter than she'd ever been and super relaxed.

Should she be ashamed this was so easy for him? He languidly kissed her, running his hand up and down her back, but his fingers—Oh God, those fingers at her center.

He circled her clit, then slid through her slick heat like he was purposely prolonging her explosion. No fumbling. No bumbling. He was deliberate.

"Malcolm," she whimpered, riding the sharp edge of pleasure from his touch and pain from her bruises, and not wanting to tip on either side. This felt exquisite. Just like the male under her.

"Tell me what you need," he whispered.

"You know what I need." And he did. It seemed they both needed it and had been avoiding it since they first met. An idea that sounded foolish only a day ago was coming to fruition on an old basement couch.

Her body had a mind of its own and Malcolm read it perfectly. She rode his hand, lifting her torso, dropping her head back.

"Yes." Her breath hitched, but she hissed, "*Yes.*"

This promised to be the strongest orgasm of her life and he was dangling it out of her reach—because she wanted him to. Dammit, if this was a dream, then she was going to stay trapped in it as long as possible.

He changed his angle, slicking through her folds and thrusting a finger inside while circling her clit with his thumb.

Her shout that bounced off the basement walls shocked her as much as instantly slamming into her peak. Her body tensed, every muscle, and then stars exploded behind her eyes. Heat flooded from her and she rocked over his hand, milking every second out of the longest orgasm of her life.

When she sagged, he drew her close, burying his face in the crook of her neck and shoulder. "*Fuck*, bunny. That was magnificent."

"Thanks," she mumbled, straightening herself over him, and dropping one foot to the floor. She had the strongest urge to run to her room and hide. This type of experience didn't happen to her, but it likely happened to him all the time. He'd opened her up like no one else and now she was exposed and raw. Insecurity dogged her.

"Don't—" He groaned and his hands dug into her hips. "I'm going to come in my pants if you keep wiggling around like that."

That made her stop. He was that close? Because of her?

His eyes were slits, concentrating, but still watching her. "Care to tell me why you seem like you were going to run away? I don't chase females, but I seem to be making a lot of exceptions for you."

The warmth his words injected her with calmed her enough to relax. She was still perched over the massive erection straining against his jeans.

She hadn't known him for long, but she only knew him as being honest. "Just stupid reasons."

"They seem real, not stupid."

"It's all the usual insecure stuff most women deal with. Only amplified, because...you."

His brows lifted. His hips rocked up and his lips thinned as he visibly held himself still. "Because I'm not like you."

"You and everyone you've been with, I'm sure." Shifters had extraordinary senses, lifespans, and lifestyles. She was boring old Patience Montgomery. She milked her goat, fed her chickens, and collected cats and dogs that wound up lost and injured on her property. She sighed. "I can't do this and then just turn away when you hit up Tamera, or someone like her."

A line formed between his brows. "I don't want to be with Tam." Realization lit his eyes. "I don't want to be with her." He looked at her like she told him the secret to solving a Rubik's cube. A laugh rumbled through his chest and under her hands. "What a relief, Patience. I don't want that female anymore. I don't feel drawn to her. She's almost a stranger."

"Didn't you two…"

"Yes. When we were teens." He relaxed into the cushions, but under her, he was hard as granite. "And since I saw her, I've been wondering, what now? Do I have to mate her? What does it mean that Darius died? But I don't feel it. I don't feel like I belong to her." He noticed her confusion. "We're inexorably drawn to our mates. It helps, you know, get the ball rolling. But not many of us have been in my situation."

"Okay, so not Tamera." What a relief, but she was a realist. It's what made her good at her job, both in knowing how to help their clients, and how much she was able to since she wasn't a counselor or mental health professional. She was a life coach, at best, and an uncertified one at that. "But you go to places like Razor's Edge and stuff."

She couldn't compete, not with the partners he found there, and not with that lifestyle.

He sighed and brushed her cheek with his thumb. "You remember what Tam said the other day? About me leaving a bunch of unsatisfied females?"

She nodded.

"Tam was my first, and I thought my only. Then she was gone. My brother and I went off to do what we were supposed to do, but we'd each lost someone and…" His eyes flickered. "And we didn't want to admit how cold and unloving our home had become after Camille vanished. So we partied and we fucked and it was always together. For everything."

117

It took her a moment to clarify what he said. "Oh. Like ménage."

His lips quirked. "At a minimum."

"Oh." She couldn't be jealous of a lifestyle she couldn't fathom. Could she be any more boring to him? There was a soap closet behind her for God's sake. That was the height of her weekend entertainment.

"And then Harrison found a mate, which we thought was impossible. Then it was just me. My father's in prison. Did you know that? He was part of our former government. The negligent part. He could get out, but he stays there, avoiding Maw."

He'd lost his mate and most of his family, and eventually his brother found someone to spend his life with. "You're lonely."

"Not just that. I'm…in a new place in life. I tried living my old life, the one Harrison and I used to have, and it's unfulfilling. I think that's why I have to find my sister. I can't move on until I know what happened."

"Can't. Or won't?" She'd helped plenty of females—humans and shifters alike—escape many situations. Forced marriages. Controlling home life. Emotional abuse. He might not be able to find Camille for a very good reason—because she didn't want to be found.

"Can't, Patience. Don't you think learning what happened is important?"

"Yes, but you don't need to roam aimlessly in order to do it. Then it's just an excuse."

He let out a long breath and skimmed his hands over her, dipped his fingers under the hem of her sweater and wicked them up her body. "Patience. You're not afraid to tell it like it is."

She was afraid to tell him a lot. Like how what she did for a living wasn't limited to humans. How much she cared for him when they'd only known each other since Friday. And that she was only terrified of losing her memories because he'd be gone, too.

"The point to this humbling confession," he said in a husky voice, "is that I've been lost for months. I haven't been able to be with anyone and get off. I haven't been able to sate my needs on my own. But on this couch, with you, I had to fight not to climax when you came all over my hand."

A shiver coursed down her spine.

"And even though I just talked about the most depressing shit of my life and how ashamed I am that I can't get it together and just be happy for my brother, I can think of nothing more than you, and making you shout my name again."

Her lips parted. This was too good to be true. She didn't have an answer for why they fit together, only that they did. She didn't know for how long, so she'd live in the moment.

She rocked against him. The erection that had flagged returned. She sat back on his thighs and worked the clasp of his pants, undoing first the button, then slowly lowering the zipper like she was opening a gift she'd been anticipating her whole life.

The broad tip peeked out. Her body thrummed, looking forward to this more than anything, ever. It wasn't just the physical aspect. They'd both bared their souls, the part of themselves they didn't show to anyone. It made this real. What happened between them meant something, even if neither understood what.

As she bared each inch, she could only think of all the ways this could play out. Should she use her mouth first? Her hands? A combo?

She'd given blow jobs before, but they were mostly for practice, not because she truly enjoyed the experience. She'd just wanted to know what it was like and how to do them.

But with Malcolm, she was giddy at the opportunity to have something so magnificent all to herself, and shaking with need and trepidation.

How rough would he be? Would he be gentle like he was earlier? What did he need?

She was about to find out when her brother's worried voice rang from the top of the stairs. "Patience. Where are you? God, I just heard. Are you okay?"

MALCOLM ZIPPED up his dick so fast, he pinched the skin. The pain would've dropped him any other time, but it was the more desirable outcome compared to being caught with his cock waving in the face of this guy's sister.

"I'll be right up." Patience scrambled off him, an adorable blush cresting over her cheekbones. She tugged at her clothing until it didn't look like he'd been copping feels wherever possible.

He sat up, wincing at the agony of the seam of his fly digging into his hard-on.

Couldn't get it hard for weeks without major stimulation and now he couldn't get it to go away.

The greedy way Patience looked at it was more than a male could ask for. She hadn't looked like she was hungry for what he could do for her, but what she could do to him. And he'd wanted to know. More than anything in his life, he wanted to know what she wanted to do to him.

"You're okay?" Jacob's relieved voice slashed into his thoughts, but thankfully the brother stayed put upstairs. "Lord, when the police contacted me, I rushed straight here."

Patience tossed him an apologetic—and regretful—smile over her shoulder and jogged upstairs. Her voice faded as she drew Jacob farther into the house and away from catching them together on the couch.

Malcolm sat up and scrubbed his face. What the hell was he doing? Patience was his job. He might have to scrub her mind. She might still be hiding stuff that was pertinent to his life and the safety of his people. But none of that had mattered when she lay in his arms.

None of that had mattered when she was in danger. He would fight for her and this little spot of tranquil paradise and her menagerie of animals.

All the furniture was still askew. He could fix that before he went upstairs. Then he'd go up there and do his job. Talk to Jacob, get a sense for what he knew and what he was hiding.

Fixing the furniture gave his dick enough time to go down, but he had to take his time.

Patience coming apart in his arms—

Blood coursed back down to his groin. He sucked in deep breaths and rearranged the couch and checked the soap closet.

Travis hadn't destroyed any of her hard work. If he had, Malcolm would be too tempted to track him down and beat him for every bar of soap he damaged.

Finally, he was ready to meet Jacob.

He followed the voices. They were in the living room.

"...if he hadn't been here." Defensiveness laced Patience's tone.

"But Brenden and Delia showed up."

"Yeah, they heard my yells. But what if they hadn't?"

"I still don't like it."

Malcolm stood on the kitchen side of the entryway. Jacob had to know he could hear. Malcolm studied him. A few inches shorter than him, Jacob had darker hair that brushed the tops of his ears and a surprisingly defined physique for a guy with an office job. Despite that, he had an approachable air, a persona that drew others to him instead of scaring them away. The siblings had that in common. Jacob's hands were in his pockets and he wasn't towering over his sister trying to intimidate her into doing what he wanted. Concern emanated from him.

He seemed like a caring brother.

The human finally noticed him and drew himself straighter.

Patience's cheeks were still tinted, but instead of dropping her gaze, she gave her brother a straightforward introduction. "Jacob, this is Malcolm."

Jacob didn't make a move to shake hands. "Thanks for helping my sister."

"Don't mention it. Glad I was here." To think, if he'd been farther away and hadn't heard her scream. He repressed a shudder.

"Why are you here, again?" Jacob asked, his tone as sharp as his gaze.

Patience told him, she said she had. But sure, he'd play along. "I have to know why—"

"Yeah, I know why you're here, but why *here*, in this house?"

Patience rolled her eyes. "Jacob."

Jacob ignored her, his gaze zeroed in.

Malcolm had the urge to sneer, but he reminded himself that Jacob was worried about some strange shifter invading his sister's life. "It's easier to make a cover story when people ask who I am and what I'm doing here, which we haven't had to do yet because I'm at the farm, miles out of town and only the neighbors know I'm here."

"And Tamera." Patience made a disgruntled noise. "Who I guess is a neighbor now?"

"Tamera?" Jacob's forehead furrowed. "Like, Taunting Tamera?"

Patience's lips pursed and she only nodded, not spilling any of his story.

He might as well. "She was supposed to be my mate, once upon a time. But that's over." And what a relief to finally say it. Would he go as far as to say he dodged a bullet? Would they have been happy, or would he have gone through life thinking she was the shit and everyone else was too sensitive? Would she have been as miserable as she feared?

They would've been like his parents.

Jacob's inspection of him changed to one that held even less respect than before. "Over?" He sounded doubtful.

"Would *you* marry her?" Malcolm asked seriously.

Jacob shrugged, like *point taken*. But Malcolm hated that he sensed Jacob didn't believe him because Tamera was a sexpot and his sister wasn't.

Jacob definitely didn't need to know that Patience was indeed a wanton sexpot. No one else needed to know but him.

"I'm okay with him here, Jacob," Patience said, her tone heavy with warning. She hated to be coddled and treated like she couldn't take care of herself. She might not be so defensive if she was shown more respect by those close to her, like her coworkers.

Brenden and Delia seemed like they were good, but with Tamera staying there, he hoped they stayed far away. Patience had enough to deal with.

"He's been a big help. And I don't think Dot would forgive me if I kicked him out."

Jacob's face morphed into disbelief. "Your crabby goat?"

"She's putty in his hands." Her cheeks reddened again.

Malcolm was fine keeping his mouth shut about who else was putty in his hands, except to say, "The cats like me, too."

"The cats..." Jacob shook his head. "Whatever, you two obviously have an understanding." He faced his sister. "But don't forget for one moment that he'll be ordered to tamper with that brain of yours—and mine, too."

"Then tell me why," Malcolm said.

Jacob jerked his gaze up to him. "Why what?"

"Why it's so important that you two know about us? Why do all the shifters around here who know that you know look the other way?" Malcolm steadied his stare on both of them. "Your grandmother told stories and I'm going to read between the lines and guess she knew, too. Your parents?"

Anxiety infused the air stronger than any Febreze air freshener. Wasn't that interesting? Their parents were dead. Why would they be concerned he was asking about them?

"Yes," Patience answered. "They knew."

"So," Malcolm said, "decades of shifters not caring if humans knew. Decades of the authorities not being notified, not even an anonymous tip. Why?"

To be honest, he was glad no one had notified their authorities before the overturn of the government. In those days, Guardians were sparse and overworked. If the wrong leaders found out, Jacob and Patience would've been killed with efficiency cited as the reason.

The siblings fidgeted as they stared at him.

Jacob folded his arms. "It's just how it is in Twin Forks. They trust us and we help them out."

Malcolm hooked on the last part. "Help them how?"

Patience slid a sidelong look away from her brother. "If they do something...odd...we come up with excuses."

"And the shifters can't do that themselves?"

The siblings exchanged a look with each other and Malcolm was suddenly grateful that they couldn't mind-speak.

Patience answered. "Well, they don't always talk around the shifters. There are gossipers."

Jacob nodded. "Small town."

He eyed them, suspicion mounting each second. They weren't lying, he couldn't smell it. But they weren't being honest and forthcoming. With Jacob, he expected it. But that Patience didn't trust him? That stung.

He'd been here the whole week watching out for her, and after what they'd just done in the basement... Didn't he mean more to her?

But what did he expect? He was here for work. No matter how Patience was tunneling under his skin, closer to places he hadn't inspected for a long time, this was about work.

"Fine," he bit out. "When you two decide to tell me everything, I'll be right here."

He stomped outside, leaving his heart behind.

CHAPTER 10

*M*alcolm still wasn't talking to her. It'd been another week, but so unlike the previous week when they'd shared meals and watched TV together at night. Instead, he'd stayed outside until it was her bedtime.

She'd heard his deep voice rumbling outside the door and it sent quivers through her, her body reminding her that she hadn't been filled with him like she'd wanted to be.

He was out for a run now. She was going stir crazy. If she made one more batch of soap, she'd die of insanity. He did all her chores. The animals loved him. She went to work and came home to a tidy house and laundry done. He usually had a meal made, but he'd already eaten.

She felt lonelier now than before she'd met him.

The weather was getting nicer and she could plot her garden. The soil was too cold to plant, but she could make her markers and get it all ready. It'd be something to do at the very least.

She bypassed her yellow boots and went out to the shed. Her dogs waited by a pile of clothes at the edge of the trees behind the barn. It only proved how besotted all her animals were. Malcolm could shift so close to them and they weren't fazed.

Pathetic.

She usually stayed inside while he ran to keep from invading his privacy. She'd heard they weren't modest beings, but her human self couldn't be a Peeping Tom. This past week, he stayed away so long, she'd practically put herself under house arrest. It was her day off, and she decided she would enjoy the nice day.

Grabbing her markers and making a mental tally of what she wanted to plant, she hummed to herself. She never hummed.

That male unnerved her.

Giving her the cold shoulder. Who did he think he was?

She grabbed her armload and left the shed, carefully stepping over the threshold. Turning toward the garden, movement caught her eye. She lifted her gaze.

A squeak escaped.

The biggest wolf she'd ever seen, and a unique color of chocolate brown, transformed into the most magnificent male form she'd ever seen. Strong broad shoulders sloped to a trim waist that she barely noticed as her gaze bumped over each ripple in his abdomen. *So many.*

And his... Yeah. His manhood hung thick and heavy between his powerful thighs. She barely ripped her eyes off it but her perusal was propelled by a force she had no control over. Even his calves were sexy.

Taking her time, her gaze traveled back up his body, wishing she was close enough to climb him.

Her gaze connected with his and she gulped.

"Sorry." She spun around, dropping her posts, her Sharpies, and her small stakes. "Dammit."

She dropped to pick them up. Bare feet entered her line of view.

"Need help?" He squatted next to her. Completely naked.

Of course, the first thing she saw was his dick. Her mouth went dry. "No. I'm fine. You don't need to help."

"No, I got it."

"Get dressed," she hissed.

He rested back on his feet. Or at least that's what she assumed he did from the faint scraping on the ground. She didn't dare look at him.

"This is the way of my people," he replied calmly. "And you seem to know a lot about us that you're not telling me, so I might as well walk around naked."

Her desire swelled until it was bursting out of her skin. "I don't want you to."

"I can smell your lie."

With a huff, she sat back on her feet and aimed her gaze at his eyes and only his eyes.

"Of course I'd love to look at you naked, but since you've been ignoring me for the last week, I think you're only doing it to mess with me, and that makes me angry."

"Do you know why I haven't talked to you for the last week?" The edge of his voice skated across her skin. The beam of his intense stare caught her. Was he closer? How could he move closer without unfolding that big body? "Because you gave me one of the most erotic moments of my life and then stood next to your brother and lied to me. We both know what rides on this. You forgetting me. Me having to make you forget me, and instead of being honest, you keep hiding the truth."

She snapped her mouth shut. She didn't forget his nudity, but there were so many important points to his words that her mind stayed busy working through them.

"Who's lying to whom?" she managed to get out. He didn't want her to forget him? Or he just didn't want to be the one to do it? He had a big heart, but she didn't need to be handled with pity.

"What do you mean? I haven't lied."

"I wouldn't know. I can't smell you." Her face burned. She couldn't detect his emotions by scent, but she knew his smell. After his runs, he smelled like fresh air and fir trees with a hint of musk she could roll in. "But most erotic? Come on. I don't even know you that well and I know that's not true."

"Patience, you know me better than anyone except my twin." He stated it like a fact. She almost bought it.

"We've only known each other less than three weeks."

"And we've *talked*. I don't talk to females. Or males, including my coworkers. And if you're referring to what Tam said, then yes, I have a lot of sexual experience and with more than one partner. And it's all been forgotten once I left the room and started the next day. Who I was with, what we did, all of it. Gone." His voice dropped. "But I haven't been able to quit thinking about how you felt, how you tasted, how you looked when you came."

If she dropped her gaze, she knew she'd see an erection. It couldn't hide from her peripheral vision and it only added validity to what he said.

She still couldn't believe it. "But I'm me and you're so *you*."

"I'm not special, Patience. You are."

"You are special. You're kind, but fierce. You help without expecting anything. And you're fun to talk to. When I'm around you, I don't feel like I have to pick up the load for both of us so you can go do what you want to do. I feel like your equal." She put her hand over her mouth. She was nothing but inferior to shifters, but she'd just equated herself with him.

She helped many through hard times and helped them hide from their people, with the assumption that they outdid her in every way. They could smell her emotions, they were stronger, better-looking, more courageous. And maybe she liked that they still needed her beyond that, but mostly, she just wanted to help. Because it was what she did.

But with Malcolm, she felt like more than a lifetime of obligation to those in need. She felt like she was worth more than what she could do for others. She was just Patience, who lived on her own, loved her animals, and lived for binge-watching shows.

He was next to her. "You're so much more than I am. I want you so bad. I want all of you. But I shouldn't, we shouldn't, until you talk to me."

She gazed up at him, setting her hands on the hot skin of his shoulders. She didn't have a chance to say anything.

His lip curled, revealing a sharp canine, his gaze stuck on her mouth. "But mostly, I don't fucking care because all I want to do is feel you come against me again."

Her lips parted and he captured them, crushing her with his hunger. Before she knew it, they were sprawled over the grass outside her shed. His hard length was pinned between them, but she opened herself to him, wishing that gardening in a skirt was a thing.

"Patience." He kissed his way down her neck. "I'm a starving male, and only you've been able to satisfy me."

Like on the couch, she was lost in a dream and she didn't want to wake up. She tangled her hands through his hair, letting the silky strands run through her fingers. He pushed her shirt up and licked his way up her belly. The slight breeze crested over her skin, sending shivers cascading down her back.

She wanted nothing else at this moment but to connect with him. To be together at a deeper level than they'd been able to reach before.

He used his mouth to shift her bra and free a nipple. It

peaked in the cool air before it was encapsulated by his greedy mouth.

A whole week she'd missed him, and she hadn't known him that much longer. She'd been on so many dates before, had them all fail, that she didn't want to miss this wave of passion, of need, that she felt with him.

He nipped her sensitive skin and teased her puckered flesh. She arched her back into him and ran her hands over his shoulders, down his arms, and curled her fingers back into his hair.

A faint buzzing broke into the lust-filled fog. Her phone?

Without missing a beat, he snagged it from her pocket and tossed it next to them. The choice was hers. Keep going, or answer the damn thing.

Keep going.

She widened her legs to fit him better. His hips rocked gently, frustrating her that she was to blame for the clothing between them.

Her phone kept buzzing.

She ignored it and Malcolm switched to the other nipple, his hand stroking down her belly to her waistband.

A ding that she had a message went ignored.

His fingers were almost where she craved him the most, when her phone went off again.

"For fuck's sake." She flipped it up to see who was calling. Jacob.

She hesitated. Malcolm paused.

"It's probably a New Horizons thing and there's plenty of others who can help." She was about to put the phone down when a message flashed on her screen.

Special case. Need you.

"Dammit." Her head thunked to the ground. The pestering calls and the emergency described as a special case could only mean one thing. A shifter was trying to leave her pack.

And she was going to have to lie to Malcolm to help.

HE'D NEVER HAD a case of blue balls as strong as when Patience clambered away from him, apologizing profusely but saying there was a difficult case at the center and Jacob needed help.

With his clothes back on and an unhappy erection that was thwarted a second time, he roamed the yard. The cats followed him, and the dogs, who had enough sense to leave him and Patience alone while they were getting it on, were back by his side.

His own little pack.

What packs were in and around Twin Forks? He'd been thinking on an individual shifter basis—rather, he hadn't been thinking a whole lot about the Patience issue at all. His reluctance to carry out his position with her was directly inhibiting his work.

But what if it helped him?

So he considered the problem at different angles. Were there pack leaders living in Twin Forks that condoned human knowledge and utilized it for their benefit to help their kind keep from being exposed?

If so, that'd build a strong case to leave Patience and her brother alone.

What about Brenden and Delia? He could find out what pack they were in and get a sense of who knew what. If the couple knew he was trying to help Patience, perhaps they'd open up.

He started in that direction, then stopped. Tamera.

He smiled. He smelled like blooming meadow flowers. It

was strong, like it'd been painted over him. He'd been living with Patience and of course, her scent had permeated his clothing, but this was different. The potent cloud of desire, both his and hers, oozed from him.

He'd take a shower first. Patience didn't need to be targeted by Tamera for anything more than being a human and the neighbors had to trust that he had Patience's best interest in mind and not a need to get in her pants.

Which he hadn't really been able to do yet.

He ran through the shower and picked fresh clothing to make sure he was seen as nothing more than a fair and impartial Guardian, then jogged through the few acres of trees separating the properties.

He caught a familiar scent before a light-colored wolf veered into his path.

"Tam," he said tersely.

She shifted, unfolding her strong body. He kept his gaze above the neckline and secured his mind from turning to earlier when he'd done the same in front of Patience.

"To what do we owe the honor?" She cocked her head. "Get bored with the human already? I'm surprised you lasted this long."

Ignoring her caustic comments was for the best. "I need to speak with Brenden and Delia."

Her expression flickered and she shuttered it so fast he couldn't interpret it. "They're not here. They have errands in town."

"Do you know when they'll be back?"

Tamera feathered her fingers down between the middle of her breasts. He refused to look, but truthfully, he could look his fill and that erection he'd battled earlier wouldn't make an appearance. Patience had his dick wrapped around her soap-making little fingers and she hadn't even touched him with those fingers.

"You could stay with me until they come back," she said, her voice breathy.

"No, thanks."

Tamera's back went ramrod straight. She wasn't used to being denied, and when they were younger, he didn't deny her a thing. "When was the last time you had sex?"

"None of your business, Tam."

"Razor's Edge? Please tell me you haven't fucked Rescue Rabbit and feel some sort of obligation to her."

He wearied of Tamera and her constant digs regarding Patience. "As I said, it's none of your business." He'd ask her to pass on to the others that he was looking for them, but he doubted the message would make it.

He turned to go, but Tamera slipped in front of him, her expression grave. "Look, Mal. Don't mistake this for any affection toward those humans or anything. I like Twin Forks. If you stay and keep poking around, you're only going to hurt those you seem really apprehensive about hurting."

"Patience and Jacob?"

"There's…" She looked around, her gaze touching on the trees, one at a time. "This place has been the only real home I've known. I get it, I'm kind of a bitch by human standards." He cocked a brow and she scowled at him. But yeah, she was pretty tame compared to many others he'd crossed, thanks to his job. "But catty or not, I can be me here. Darius is gone but that doesn't mean I'm farmed out to the next eligible male in order to create some bullshit pack alliance."

His brows drew together. "If you're getting forced…"

"Then what, Mal? Tell someone? What do you think my father would've done? He almost—" She drew back and rolled her lips in.

"He almost what?"

Her shoulders sagged and she folded her arms across her breasts, her expression vulnerable in a way he'd never seen before. "When he found out that not only was I mating Darius, but leaving Tame Peaks, he almost killed Darius."

He tried to read between the lines to figure out what she was saying. "You mated Darius *because* he was leaving Tame Peaks?"

"Yes. Remember my ability?"

He thought back to their talks when he did most of the talking. Had she said anything about an ability?

"I don't think I gave you a chance to tell me."

She gave him a look that said she wasn't surprised. "I can tell when two people are compatible. I can tell when they're natural mates, and I can tell when they'd work together. I knew Darius and I would be compatible, and more than that, when we talked, we both dreamed of getting away from pack life, from our lives being dictated by what we could do for others and not ourselves."

"It wasn't like that—"

"You and Harrison knew what you had to do with your lives and you were fine with it. But pretend for a second that you didn't. Do you think you could've gone off to do something like interpretive dance, or that Harrison could've taken up wood carving?"

"Why would we—"

"Your mother would've made sure you each mated someone of her choosing. She would've made sure you worked with or for your father. She would've used you to secure her power in the pack and I would've been nothing but a pawn at her disposal. It wouldn't have mattered where we moved. If I mated you, I'd be nothing but a tool for the Lycan Council, and I don't care if they've been dissolved. You're still a tool for the Synod, at their beck and call. What would they have allowed me to do? Live closely and behave myself until they found me useful. And if you didn't think twice about that, then that was part of the problem."

No, he hadn't thought twice. That was the way it was done. Most shifters wanted power and to prove that power.

Most. But not all. And the younger generations, like him and Tamera, had more connections with the outside world, with social media, with humans who had the freedom to be who they wanted to be wherever they wanted to be.

A minor part of his work was policing those shifters, making sure they didn't risk exposure, ensuring they were part of a pack. Mostly, he dealt with shifters going rogue or feral or being generally abusive and disruptive to the harmony of the pack.

Shifters like Tamera, if she hadn't worked around the rules and mated with Darius.

"What pack are you a part of here?"

Alarm flashed in her eyes. "The same one Darius joined when we moved here."

"Okay, and which one is that?" Packs were often made of families and carried the same name as the leader.

"Why do you need to know? You're not investigating me."

He shrugged. "I sort of am. I need to know why shifters here are operating outside of the rules." Even if it's in a minor way, it could clue him in to major problems.

She regained her composure but her scent was all sorts of uncomfortable. "Brenden, Delia, and I are protective of our pack. We don't want outsiders butting in."

He studied Tamera. Gone was the wicked seductress and in its place was the half-panicked mate who stomped all over his heart when they were younger. "What's going on here, Tam?"

Her jaw tensed. "Nothing, if you leave it alone. Otherwise, a lot of us are going to get hurt."

What the hell? Never in his career had he been blocked from talking to a pack leader. It wasn't like they were in charge of the colony. They were more like the head of the family.

"If you don't talk to me, I'm going to have to comb through this town and interview every single shifter I come across."

Her eyes widened. She ran a hand through her hair and marched to her clothing. He averted his eyes while she got dressed.

"You don't understand, Malcolm. How could you? You're a Guardian. If you had your way, you'd enslave me, or worse, put me in front of the Synod to be imprisoned, if they don't condemn me."

He shook his head. "What the hell are you talking about?"

"Us, Mal." Fear lined her face. He'd never seen her like this before. "All of us here. We're all the ones who got away and we live free. If you step in and do your job, you're not only going to ruin it, but you're going to hurt all of us." She hugged herself. "Rescue Rabbit, too."

He still didn't understand what she was saying, but he got the message loud and clear. Something was going on. Something Tamera was involved in. Probably the neighbors too. Patience and her brother. That was why they were protected in a weird sort of way. Something his kind would find illegal, and something he'd have to deal with in an official capacity.

"Spell it out, Tam. Help me understand."

Her lower lip trembled and she gave him a guarded look he only got dealing with victims when he was trying to get information to go get the bad guy. Only after what she said, he felt like the bad guy in this case.

"I'm talking about those of us who fit into our own society. Those of us who want to live as free as humans do. It's not fair when you think about it. We live so much longer, why are they the only ones who get to enjoy freedom?"

Others would argue that it's because of shifters' enhanced

strength and abilities. Give them an inch and they'd take the whole damn forest. There'd be a war between species, and it'd be bloody. They'd come out on top, but it'd change the world. They didn't procreate like humans, and he couldn't live in a society that embraced their inner beast and enslaved them. Most shifters liked the status quo. To live and roam among humans but retreat to their own way of life. Shifters liked their Starbucks, too.

Tamera threw a hand up. "I got away—I got away from what was basically an arranged marriage, I got away from controlling parents, I got away from an archaic way of life—which is what pack life is. I was one of the lucky ones. And it's only because of the shifters here who helped me." She pinned him with her fervent gaze. "And humans like your girlfriend Rescue Rabbit."

CHAPTER 11

*P*atience led the female through the center. They looked like they were the same age, but the female hesitantly admitted to being 114. She seemed comfortable with Jacob, but by the time Patience arrived, she was looking around like she expected something like shifter feds to break through the doors.

Her hair was still wet from swimming in the nearby river. It was the only way shifters escaped if they didn't have the ability to hide their scent. Instead, they found a river system and mapped the best way to use the water to get as close to Twin Forks as they could. The river was miles away, on the opposite side of town from Patience's place. But Rainey had run straight here.

Jacob left as soon as Patience arrived, standard practice to make their new arrival more comfortable, though it seemed like the shifter felt unusually comfortable around him.

If their new client knew about Malcolm, she'd run back to the abuse she'd been facing.

Rainey was supposed to mate a rival pack male in hopes to broker a truce. A century of hoping she found her mate in nature's due course shriveled in a moment. She said she wanted to be able to get an education and travel and enjoy life until she found a mate to do it all with.

A typical shifter case. Patience and Delia couldn't help them if they were already mated. The bond would make it too hard for the female to hide, and she'd risk all of them. Those who knew about the special help New Horizons offered only told those they knew were good candidates. They were a secret network of sympathizers and those who'd been in the same situations before.

Even Tamera knew about them and kept her mouth shut. She probably would've sought their help had she not mated. To escape her fate of mating Malcolm. The ironic circling back of all this wasn't funny.

While Rainey picked out a new outfit and some toiletries, Patience tried to think about what it would be like to know she had to mate Malcolm right out of high school. That her life would be bound to his and she'd have to follow him because his job took precedence.

It was hard to think through. Her mind stalled on mating Malcolm.

Being bound to such an honorable male, a guy who brought her supper when she worked late, and who was a total goat pushover?

She might not have minded being in that position, but Tamera did, and that was what mattered. Just because Malcolm would've treated Tamera decently didn't mean the female wouldn't have been a prisoner of birth and circumstance.

She swung her attention back to Rainey. By the time shifters arrived, they had either lost their clothes, or managed to bring one outfit with them through various swims and shifts it'd taken to flee. And if they were willing to go through all that to get away, Patience had no issues helping them.

She loved her home and would never want to leave it. To swim through rivers and run through miles and miles of forest, fearing they'd get tracked down at any moment to leave their home, meant something.

Brenden and Delia were out now, looking for a place to rent for Rainey until she earned enough to get to Freemont and live on her own.

Rainey lifted a bar of soap to her nose. "This is nice. Is it homemade?"

"I make it with only a drop of essential oil and no fake fragrance. Goat milk."

Rainey started to smile, then froze. Her expression turned to a mix of fear and betrayal. Her gaze darted around the room as she clutched her items to her chest.

"What's wro—"

"It's all right," Malcolm said from behind her. "I'm only here for information."

Patience spun around. "What—How?"

He tossed her a tempered glance, concealing what he really thought. But she got the sense he was disappointed in her.

"I'm not going back." Rainey backed around a table, her eyes frantic. She dropped her armload in a pile on the nearest table. Her knees were bent, and the way she eyed Malcolm only inspired more worry. Rainey was in fight mode.

"I just want to hear your story." Malcolm's hard gaze landed on Patience. "And then you're going to tell me *everything*."

Patience swallowed hard. "How did you know—"

"Not from you," he snapped. His expression softened when he looked at Rainey. "It's been brought to my attention that many of our kind still feel trapped by our ways, despite the change in government."

Rainey relaxed at the tone more than the words. "But you're-you're a Guardian. I've seen your picture before. You're the one with a twin."

"I'm Malcolm. Have you heard that my twin is mated to Sylva?"

Patience glanced between them.

Rainey wasn't swayed by Malcolm's announcement. "Lot of good she's done us. The Synod might've stopped the corruption but they still support our old ways."

"They do," he said. "They also support the people, and if they don't hear the stories, they won't know what's going on. What's your name?"

Rainey shifted her weight from foot to foot. "Rainey. You won't make me go back?"

Patience's hopes fell at the uncompromising look on Malcolm's face.

"I can't make promises. But I can promise I'll do everything I can to help you live the life you want."

The shifter female shook her head. "They won't listen. My pack leaders, my colony leaders? They'll tell another story. Do you expect a Synod full of males to listen to someone like me?"

"They will with my help. And Sylva's."

Patience hadn't heard anything about Sylva but Malcolm spoke of her with nothing but trust and confidence.

Rainey squared her shoulders and folded her arms. "Fine. But I can guarantee they're going to think I'm nothing but a foolish, spoiled female. I'm an artist, and I travel to Freemont to sell my paintings in one of their galleries. I make enough to cover my expenses and live on my own." She lifted her chin. "But the powers that be say that's not good enough. I have to earn my place on my back. They won't let me move to Freemont. They won't let me find a mate on my own. They want to whore me off to another pack. Alliance, they say. What a joke. As if my pussy's so powerful it can unite a bunch of shifters who'd rather snarl at each other than have a civil conversation."

Malcolm gave a slow nod, his expression introspective. "Can you give me time, Rainey, before you run again? Can you give me time to find out how many there are like you, how many need to go to the Synod to help them get their life back?"

"As if you think the Synod will let us be free of a pack."

Patience didn't live in their world, but she knew the basic law. Always belong to a pack. Always. Helping shifters avoid pack life was her biggest crime.

"It's dangerous not to," he said.

Rainey snorted and flung an arm out to gesture around her. "There's an entire population in and around Twin Forks that are packless. We've been lied to our whole lives. It's absolutely possible, and this place proves it."

Realization dawned over Malcolm's face. Patience cringed as he spared her a glance brimming with comprehension and withering disappointment. She was helping his kind violate one of the most important laws of his kind, the one he'd worked to uphold his entire life.

"I can assure you, we haven't been lied to. I've dealt with enough shifters out of their mind—"

"They were already unstable," Rainey slashed her hands through the air. "They lost their mind and then left a pack. We're not like that. We just want to be free to *live*."

Malcolm tried to hold his expression back showing that he didn't agree with her, but Patience appreciated that he didn't say anything. "Just tell me everything and promise you won't run while I gather more information. The more shifters we have who can testify to how their packs have treated them, the better it will look to the Synod." When Rainey didn't reply, he pressed on. "You're on the run already, and it'll be worse if you run from a Guardian. I promise I'll do what I can to help you, but it'll be hard to keep that promise if you're not even here."

Rainey shot a beseeching look toward Patience. She didn't know what to do, and frankly, neither did Patience. Malcolm was their only chance.

"You can stay here until it's over," Patience offered the frightened shifter. "There's a room in the back with a bathroom and a little kitchenette. It's all stocked and ready." She met Malcolm's steely gaze and a part of her shriveled inside. She'd made life hard for him. But he'd just done the same to her.

"I'll wait here," he ground out.

She got Rainey settled. The shifter didn't say anything until Patience turned to leave. "I'm only staying because you're just as scared as I am."

"I'm sorry. I thought he didn't know." She shrugged. "I tried to keep it from him as long as I could."

Rainey spun in a circle, studying the room. "I wouldn't stay, but he cares about you and we're both kind of in this together."

"We're not a couple."

Rainey cocked a brow and Patience shut her mouth. She tried again. "I don't know what we are, but I'd like to believe that he'll do everything he can to help."

Rainey's assessing gaze didn't leave her. "He'd better. It's going to be bad for me if I have to go back, but I'll survive. Once surrounding packs find out what's been going on here, it won't matter if you remember us or not—they'll rip you apart and make everyone you love suffer."

∾

Patience looked shaken once she returned to the supply room.

"What?" he asked, irritated that he cared so much. "Did Rainey do something to you?"

She shook her head. "Just reminded me what's at stake."

Now that he knew how deep this whole thing went—years and several shifters escaping packs to never be heard from again—it wasn't only her mind on the line. There were many who'd want bloody retribution from any human who thought to meddle in shifter affairs.

They'd play with her like a cat with a ditch mouse, then they'd make her suffer. Killing her would be a mercy.

Her brother would face the same fate for helping shifters stay rogue.

This was a fucking mess.

"We should talk in Jacob's office," she said. "I called Brenden and Delia. They already heard that you knew. I'm guessing from Tamera."

He nodded once. "She didn't tell me to be vindictive. I think she really wanted me to understand."

"Not vindictive." Patience's chuckle sounded humorless. "I'd never pair that phrase with her."

She trudged from the room like the weight of the world settled solidly on her shoulders. Only, it was the fate of Twin Forks and all the shifters she'd helped over the years.

Slumping behind the desk in an office that smelled like the aftershave her brother wore, she stared at the cluttered surface.

He leaned against the doorway, resisting the urge to go to her and offer some form of comfort. A shoulder rub, a forehead massage…an orgasm.

Her effect on him was stronger than he thought. He should be pissed, and he was, but he was more concerned about how to get safely on the other side of this scenario, and if it took setting her up on some unnamed island with twenty years' worth of supplies, he'd do it.

And it'd cost him everything. He could just get a prison cell next to his father to spend eternity in.

"New Horizons is a family business, remember?" she said, leaning forward and rubbing circles over her temples. "My grandma helped a few shifters, then when my mother started the center, she used the same services to aid those in need— no matter the species. There weren't many and there was a lull after Dad—after we lost Dad. Then Jacob took over and word got out that we were back at it, but it was a rare case. It's only been recently that we seem to get one or two shifters a year looking for a new start."

That was in line with what Malcolm had noticed when he traveled from colony to colony. The younger shifters weren't as content living under strict pack law. They'd rather post the steak they were having for dinner on social media with **#raremeat** and move on.

He couldn't blame them. Wasn't that why he and Harrison were just fine leaving for the Guardians? They could travel and had little oversight as long as they did their jobs.

"How do you help them?" he asked.

"We hear their story. Brenden and Delia get them a place to live and counsel them on all things human. If they think the shifter can blend with society, they help them go to wherever they choose. Many stay here."

"And there's no pack in charge?"

She lifted a shoulder. "That's not my area. I help with the transition. They come here hungry and ragged from fleeing their pack. Most of them are terrified and paranoid, and Jacob and I know how to deal with that. It's not like we can turn them over to one of our counselors."

At least that limited the number of people involved. "Who

have you helped, Patience? I need all their names. I need to talk to every one of them."

Patience's stricken expression made his stomach sink. She couldn't or wouldn't give him that information. "We don't keep records. Nothing on paper and definitely nothing is digital. We give them a hand and they move on."

He stuffed his hands through his hair and faced the other wall. *"Fuck.* Don't you know they could've bitten that hand off? Do you have any idea what you've been messing with?"

"I have some idea."

"And that story you told me about when you were kids?"

"Mostly true, but I was too young to go searching the woods with Jacob when that shifter took our chickens."

"And where is she now?"

"I don't know."

There it was again. That sense that she wasn't telling him everything. He stomped to the desk and slammed his hands down.

She jumped and pressed back in the chair, her eyes wide, her face pale.

"Dammit, Patience. You have to tell me everything or I can't help you."

Tears gathered in her eyes and her lower lip quivered. She was the one lying but he was the one who felt like month-old dog shit.

A hot tear slipped past her eyelid and down her cheek. "She's my dad's mate, okay?"

He rocked back a few steps. *"What?* Your dad? I thought he was—" He clamped his lips shut. She never said he died. Wiley, frustrating little human. That explained why she didn't keep his obituary—it wasn't real. "Tell me the story."

"She came and found us one day. Dad was running the clinic and they...fell in love, which terrified her more. But eventually, they mated and we were all happy for a few months until his car went off a bridge."

"And then your dad had to disappear before people questioned why he healed so fast." Because as the human mate of a shifter, he'd get their healing abilities, too. That explained Patience's knowledge and comfort around shifters better than anything.

"I don't know where he's at, I swear. Not even Jacob does. He only knows how to reach him in case of emergency."

"Was I an emergency?" he asked quietly.

She nodded, her eyes gleaming with guilt.

He let out a long breath. "What's their names?"

"My dad's name is Paul and we've always called her Millie but Dad never told us her real name. Said it was safer for us if we never knew." Her watery gaze met his. "I never ask for their real names. I tell them to give me the new name they want to go by."

"You could get tortured for that information."

"And I wouldn't be able to give them up," she said simply.

Self-sacrificing fucking woman. "Why? Why do all this?"

She shrugged again. "It's what I'm good at. I mean, if you want to dig deeper, I'm sure you can say that oh, my mom did this and it's a way to feel close to her since she died when I was a baby. But it's my life. It's always been my life. My parents are gone. Grandma's gone. It's all I have."

She's needed. The ones she rescued needed her, people looking for a new start needed her. It was her identity. It'd be a good one if she hadn't delved into the fucking shifter world.

"Have Jacob get a hold of your dad. Tell him what's going on, that I want to help, and that I need to talk to his mate." And he'd have to call the commander.

He trusted his boss, but he also wanted to apprise Sylva of the situation as soon as possible. The leaders of the Synod were quality people he trusted, but this could cause a rift between their people and their government and they hadn't fully recovered from the last time that happened.

"I'll follow you back to your house." Would he have to check her phone again? See who she called?

"I can't leave until Jacob gets back. One of us has to stay here when we have a client and since she's a shifter..."

Right. She couldn't call in her coworkers and dump a work shift on them like they did to her.

"You're not staying." He wanted her at the house. "I doubt your dad is going to traipse through town when everyone who knew him thinks he's dead. He'll go to your place?"

She nodded and curled in on herself. "Do you think there's a chance your government will side with them?"

He took a moment to think it over. Unlike the people here, he'd be honest. "No. Sides in this case, in all these cases, won't help anything. Our kind is struggling to modernize and adapt to this world while keeping our presence a secret. It might bring changes, but those changes won't come easily."

"Does your kind really go crazy if they don't have a mate, or belong to a pack?"

"Yes." He flexed his jaw. He'd dealt with too many, so crazed you'd swear they were rabid, and just like rabies, there was no getting better. "Going without a mate for too long, definitely. I've seen it a hundred times, and it's as bad or worse than you've heard. Leaving a pack?" He rolled his shoulders and thought about what Rainey said. "It's a chicken and egg deal. Most usually aren't mated. So, yeah, they've decided they're lone wolves and they leave, or they leave and slowly sink into insanity because they don't meet their mates since they avoid our societies. Usually, it means they think they're above the law and act accordingly. Either way, it's caused a lot of pain and death for all involved."

He shoved another hand through his hair and peered

down the hallway. Jacob wasn't back yet. "I'm going to make a few calls. Give me Brenden's number. I'll start with him when I'm done."

She looked away. Would she refuse? Go down swinging for the ones she cared about? Where did he fit in on that spectrum, or had he fallen off it as soon as he'd shown up?

CHAPTER 12

*P*atience concentrated on the road. The sun was setting, and while the days were getting longer, this felt like the longest of the year. The longest of the decade. Of her whole life.

The hurt in his eyes.

She wanted to trust him, but she was determined to do her job and he was set to do his. They were each irrevocably tied to what they did for a living.

She maneuvered a curve, a few miles yet to go when movement in the ditch caught her attention. A lifetime of instinct made her stop. This wasn't a big lump like when she found Malcolm. Just a flurry of the dried grasses sticking up from the side of the road that told her it was more than the wind.

It could've been a wild animal, and if so, it'd be gone by the time she got out.

She stopped the car and left the engine running. When she got out, she skirted to the edge of the road. She knew she wasn't dealing with anything human, but she used a soft voice when she called, "Hello?"

A slight mew greeted her.

A cat.

She started in that direction. Cats getting dumped outside of town was nothing new. She didn't question the why, just dealt with the consequence.

"Kitty, kitty, kitty." She crept closer, not wanting to scare it away. It was either injured or comfortable with humans if it made noise.

She found it. An orange tabby that looked hungry and haggard and refused to leave her spot. Because six kittens surrounded her belly.

"Look at you, mama cat," she crooned and squatted by the cat. The kittens were tiny, probably not more than a week old. Too many mouths for someone to feed if they dumped them all out here.

Going back to her car, she dug out a blanket. The task of gathering mama cat and kittens wasn't hard. Likely a house cat that was never fixed and had more babies than anticipated, or the owners just couldn't face giving another litter away.

The why didn't matter, and it was actually a relief. There were no legal consequences for helping a stray cat. Nothing like the mess she was in. She tucked them on the floor of the back seat with promises of food and water in a few minutes.

It was difficult reconciling the hard male who came to the center who was so bitterly disappointed in her with the guy who couldn't seem to get enough of her just before she left for the case.

She hadn't had time to figure out what it all meant when it didn't matter anymore. She was back to being nothing but a hard case he had to deal with.

She parked in her normal spot and gave each dog long scratches behind the ears. Her outside cats sniffed her all over as she walked to the garage to find a box to carry her rescues into the house. By the time she exited the garage, Malcolm stood on the porch, his arms crossed, making his biceps bulge.

He looked at her like he hadn't thought she'd actually come home, and the fact that she did made him question her intentions. There was no reason to stay away. After telling him about Dad, she had nothing else to hide from him and he was their only bridge to keeping this situation from being a nightmare.

She didn't speak to him, just went to the back door of her car and gathered her findings up.

She backed out. Her ass hit a hot wall behind her and she jerked upright, nearly dropping her armload.

"I've got it." He saved the box from shaking the occupants while she tried to steady it. Frowning, he peered inside. "Do animals in need just jump out at you waving signs?"

"I've learned to see the signs." She closed the car door and chattered while she walked into the house. "I have some extra bowls for food and water and an extra litter box. I'll get her set up in the spare room downstairs so she's closed off from the other cats but has some room to roam."

Malcolm didn't say anything but complied with all her directions. He fetched the bowls and filled them with soft food and water. She set up mama cat in the corner of the room with extra blankets for padding in the box. When they were done, she closed the door. He hovered behind her, standing like he had on the porch.

She couldn't face him yet. "I, uh, have to wash my hands."

She took the stairs fast enough that she hoped he wasn't right behind her, getting her jiggly ass in his face. She kept going, all the way up to her bathroom. Keeping her head down, she washed her hands.

A strong arm reached over her and pumped the soap.

Startled, she glanced up, catching his glittering eyes in the mirror.

With the light off and only residual light from behind the window blinds making it in, his irises glittered metallic, like a predator's. He was a predator. Working with them made it easy to forget their wild side. How they each carried an animal inside of them.

She'd seen that powerful body shift forms. She knew he wasn't human. And she didn't care.

She wished she could go back to that morning after she found him. When he didn't know she had secrets and she hadn't realized what he was. They were just Patience and Malcolm.

"I'm sorry," she said, unable to take her gaze off his inhuman one.

"Why?" His breath wafted across her neck as he rinsed his hands. Both of his arms were around her as he shut the water off.

"I wish we weren't on different sides of this."

He held her gaze. "If you keep thinking of this as sides, then we'll never move forward."

"That's going to be hard."

He spun her around, his hands on her waist, and leaned his forehead against hers. "Yeah. It's going to be."

"Are you all right?" She cupped his face, his beard soft against her hand.

"I will be. I just keep thinking... About all those families out there, missing a loved one, worrying that the worst happened, when that person just ran off to live a better life." His shadowed expression turned tortured. "I always feared something awful happened to my sister, but what if we were the awful that happened to her?"

"Oh, Malcolm. I wish I knew your sister and could help you."

"I don't want to think about it. I don't want to think about any of it. The shit's going to hit a big huge fan soon, and for now, I just want to get lost in your body and not think about how you don't trust me enough."

"You wouldn't be here if I didn't trust you."

His eyes searched hers. "When I'm with you, Patience…"

She waited for him to finish, but he only traced his finger along her lower lip, then down her chin, her neck, and over her chest.

No more words were needed. He tilted her head up and dropped his mouth to hers. The hunger in his touch was staggering, making her knees weak.

Like he sensed he robbed her of strength, he picked her up, his hands gripping her ass. She wound her legs around his waist as he carried her into her bedroom. They didn't break their kiss until he laid her on the bed.

"Turn your fucking phone off." He did the same with his and tossed it on her nightstand. "I locked the damn door and I'm taking my time with you, no interruptions."

She nodded, her head against her sheets. She hadn't made the bed this morning and he had her laid out on the messy side.

"Good. I want to do nothing more than drive into your sweet body, but I'm taking my time. You're my prey, bunny, and I'm playing with you."

Her breath caught. This was too much, such a sudden shift from what he'd been only a few hours ago.

He paused, sensing her uncertainty.

"Why the change?" she asked. "Why me?"

He was on his hands and knees, looming over her. "Because, bunny, you make me feel like me for once. I've been a twin my whole life. I've been a son who had to live up to a parent. I've been a Guardian. You make me feel like being nothing more than Malcolm is okay."

"Because Malcolm is pretty special."

He dropped a sweet kiss on her lips. "So tell me, why me?"

"Are you kidding? Look at you." His lips lifted with his amusement, but she didn't miss the deeper need inside of him. He needed her honesty. "But it's more than your looks. You don't expect anything of me that I don't give, and you accept everything about me. It's not about what I can do for you, but what I can do along with you."

And that was why her dating life had failed over and over. She wasn't pretty enough. She wasn't sexy enough. She was too independent. She wasn't what they wanted. Unlike Malcolm, she didn't fit the role others wanted from her. Her coworkers used her and she had no friends. Animals were better company.

"You have a good heart," she continued. "We're so different, but you accept all of me, just as I am."

He hooked fingers in the waistband of her plain black leggings and caught her gaze. "Have you told me everything?"

"Yes." Finally, she could answer him without hesitation. "You know everything about me."

He gave one firm nod before ripping her bottoms off in one smooth motion. His greedy gaze ate her up. "Take your shirt off."

He sat back on his heels and watched her, watched every part of her, hissing "*Yesss*" when she was completely bared to him.

She let him make all the first moves. He ran his hands up and down her body, as if he couldn't go on if he didn't feel every inch of her first. Then he pushed her knees up and out. Thankful for the sunset casting her room in shadows, she tried not to think about how much better he could see in the dark than her.

He got off the bed, reached behind him, and yanked his

shirt over his head. Then his pants were off. He moved swiftly and efficiently and now she cursed the darkness in the room that concealed his magnificent body.

She reached for him, but a low growl cut her off.

"I've been in pain since I met you. Let me have this."

She reclined back, her fingers trailing over her chest. He tracked the movement as he shoved her blankets out of the way to give them more room. Settling himself between her legs, he met her gaze one last time.

She saw his unasked question. Once he started, he didn't want to stop—and she didn't want him to, either. She nodded.

He lowered his head, going straight for her clit, and feasted. She jacked her hips up, but he held her steady in his iron grasp. She arched her back off the bed and fisted her hands in the sheets.

It was way too good too fast, and even though she was the most recent of them both to have gotten off, she was at the edge.

And he held her there, turning his head, alternating between flattening his tongue and teasing her with the tip. She writhed, releasing her sheets to tangle her fingers into his hair. She'd never been this wanton before, but he made her more comfortable than she'd ever been, while being so coiled it was nearly painful.

She teetered, not climaxing, but wondering how long her heart could take it when he slid one big finger inside of her.

His name bounced off her bedroom walls and she shattered around him. Her thighs closed tight around his head and she rocked and kept going. He didn't quit, didn't let up. He milked everything out of her, until her muscles gave out and her legs dropped, boneless, to the mattress. Only then did he rise, stroking one big hand down his face.

"That was fucking amazing, bunny."

157

That nickname. He could never say it again without her body reminding her of everything he could do to her with just a few touches.

"I just...wow," she panted.

He rose again and stepped off the bed, grabbing one of her legs and gently pulling her until her butt was at the edge. "I want to watch everything."

He widened her legs and gazed down at her center. She had been sated—until he gave her that blistering look of his, the one that said he couldn't get enough of her but he'd love to die trying. His huge erection jutted out, and if this had happened before they'd started, she might've scared herself out of trying to fit him inside of her. But he was like a drug and she was addicted. After what he did to her, she wasn't worried. He'd take care of her.

He fisted himself and pumped his hand once, twice. "Do you know how long it's been since I've been able to come?" He ran his hand over the calf he still held and brushed it along her thigh. "But now I'm worried that I won't last long enough to satisfy you."

"You've already satisfied me. You did before you touched me."

A line formed between his dark brows and he looked at her like she offered him the world and then followed through with every last ocean and continent.

He lightly circled her clit once. Her hips jerked, but she met his rhythm. As she swirled her hips, he placed his blunt, wide head at her entrance and slowly pushed inside. She strained against him, wanting to take him all at once, but knowing that this first time they had to be careful, more for him than for her. If he hurt her, he'd never forgive himself.

So he kept his rhythm, each circle of her pelvis taking him deeper inside. Between her thighs, she could feel the tremor that ran through him, the shake of holding back.

When he seated himself fully, he sagged over her, rocking gently, and let out a long groan. "Heaven is hot and wet and so fucking delicious."

He helped place her heels on his shoulders and braced his hands on either side of her waist. It was a way for him to hold back, to prolong the ecstasy for himself.

"I need all night with you," he said in a ragged whisper. "Once is never going to be enough."

A tiny tendril of insecurity curled inside of her. Could she be enough for him?

"Get out of your head," he growled and pumped hard.

That chased away all coherent thought. She knew nothing but how he filled her and how he touched everything inside of her.

SWEET MOTHER EARTH, he wasn't going to last long enough to make her come again. His pride said that he had to see to her pleasure first, didn't care that her honeyed taste was still on his tongue. He ground his teeth together and stroked in and out.

She melted around him, her walls flexing and rippling around him, signaling her climax.

"Oh my God, Malcolm, I don't think I can—" A deep moan resonated from her, and heat exploded at her center.

Standing over her, he got to see everything. The way her beautiful blue gems rolled back in her head and how her mouth fell open. The look of bliss and disbelief. He put that there. He pushed her past her limits, helped her learn how much her body could be pleasured and what a shit job everyone had done before him.

Did she know that's what she did for him? That he'd never had trouble holding off a climax? That he could barely contain himself from becoming a rutting, grunting beast because she robbed him of all humanity? She took everything—and he gladly gave it to her.

Everything that happened before this? It was going to have to fucking wait. He'd been desperate for this moment since he first opened his eyes in that cold ditch and saw her curvy little body standing over him.

Her walls were fisting him, demanding everything, and he gave it. With a roar, he let his guard down and pounded into her. The breasts he had future plans for bounced as he plunged in and out.

His balls tightened, and without any more warning, his orgasm slammed into him. He went ramrod straight and released into her willing, accepting body. His release went on and on. He didn't know if he stayed silent, called her name, or shouted profanity. He locked up and let it all flood out. Months and months of lackluster sex sessions that ended in shame and discomfort. Years of trying to find that special someone who'd fit him, who'd be closer to him than his twin. Someone who'd make it hard to tell where he ended and she began.

He came and came and came, and when the wave finally passed over him, ebbing in power, he sagged.

She caught him and pulled him onto the bed next to her. Soft murmurings tickled his ear.

"That was so amazing." Her voice was as soft as she was, and he relaxed into her, but he missed the heat of her tight body already.

His eyelids shut, but he only needed a few minutes. He'd had a taste of the rarest passion fruit and he wanted to devour the whole crop.

He was a beast, after all.

She gazed up at him through lowered lids, all the blue of her eyes eaten up by her pupils. What could she see of him?

He could see all of her. Every creamy inch, and he wanted to lick them all.

"Do you want to be covered up?" she asked, then blinked when she saw that he was as hard as a slab of marble once again.

"No. I'm only getting started." He flipped her over, lifting her hips.

"Malcolm, I don't think I can…" She saw something in his gaze. Could it be his need, his desperation, his utter addiction to the way she made him feel? She bit her lower lip.

"Do you trust me?"

She rolled that lip between her teeth. "I do."

He slammed into her slick, wet channel.

"Malcolm, oh my god. How are you so hard already?" But she lifted her ass in the air, giving him all-access, and he needed it at this angle.

Again, he came earlier and harder than he could've imagined. She was breathing hard, weary from orgasm number three.

"Once more," he gasped. "Just once more and both of us can rest."

Until he needed her again. It wouldn't be long. He'd never known such pleasure. But the fact was, she was still human. He could fuck all night long and into the next day, but even if her mind was willing, her body couldn't take it.

So, the third time, he rolled her to her back and set about sampling every inch of her. There wasn't a spot she wasn't sweet, as if she'd been crafted just for his taste buds. And when he entered her again, he took his time, easing inside.

She caressed his face, kissing his mouth, little gentle pecks that were so unlike anything a female had done with him before. This was dangerous territory. Feelings were involved. They always had been, but to express the depth of them would only make the outcome of this assignment worse.

"Hey," she whispered, laying a light kiss on his nose. "Out of your head."

He focused on them. On her. How her legs framed his waist. How easily they met each other, thrust for thrust, and how even though she was so much smaller than him, they fit. They just fit. And they had from the very beginning.

Electricity raced down his spine and his ball sac drew up, but he had a perfect record. He wasn't coming without her. They had this night. He didn't know what tomorrow brought other than more shifters and more problems.

And then he felt it. That small hitch she got before she crested her peak, the way her knees drew higher and her walls closed around him. She was going to come.

And again, he fell off that edge with her, and if he could stay with her like this, together, maybe there was something for them on the other side.

CHAPTER 13

*C*hickens clucked around her feet. Patience picked up the biggest of the egg layers and stroked her hand down its silky feathers. The last few days had been close to idyllic.

Malcolm diligently interviewed her neighbors and even allowed them to contact the shifters they'd helped over the years. Many of them came forward to tell their stories. Living in secrecy and isolation took its toll on some. Others missed their families but couldn't bring themselves to trade their hard-earned freedom to contact them.

Several times, she'd seen him bent over the phone, pacing a room or through the yard as he talked with someone. She never asked. It was his business. She still had her job, and he had his. But at night—and most mornings—they came together and did everything under the sun and moon and stars. They also talked.

He told her how he had Sylva's support and that the Synod was giving him time to gather the information needed before presenting it to them. She shared how Rainey was terrified the family she was supposed to be mated to might hunt her down like a prized stag.

Patience understood the levels of power in pack life more than she ever wanted to. Might makes right was still a way of life for many.

Putting the chicken down, she closed the coop back up and went to check on her goats. Malcolm helped as much as he could, but he'd been traveling all over the county, doing interviews.

All the chores were done. Next, she'd check on the new rescues. She had a day off and it was nice not to rush through her daily duties.

Mama cat was doing fine and loved the extra pets and attention. Kittens were piled against her belly and all of them seemed healthy enough. Could Patience handle seven more cats? She had a lot of property, but her outdoor cats did a good job of mousing. No, she'd have to find them homes. Mama cat wasn't barn cat material. She was obviously an indoor cat.

Straightening into a stretch, Patience jumped when the doorbell chimed.

Her belly fluttered. She'd been in the basement when that guy Travis attacked. But he hadn't used the doorbell, and whoever was visiting had. That was a good sign.

She hurried upstairs and went to the door. When she spotted the sandy brown hair spotted with gray at the temples she whipped the door open. "Dad!"

Like she was a little girl again, she launched herself into his arms. He hardly ever came back to Twin Forks. The last time was after high school graduation. Keeping in touch wasn't easy. He didn't want to leave a paper trail or a digital trail back to him, or from them to Twin Forks. The level of protection went both ways.

He looked understandably the same. A bit taller than

Jacob, but Dad stopped aging like a human before he hit forty. He looked fitter, living off the land and getting away from the desk work at New Horizons. He and Millie lived off the grid as much as possible.

"I missed you." His voice shook. These brief reunions were hard, and she often wondered if they were a reminder that both her and Jacob's life spans were much shorter and fleeting than Dad's was now. He'd lost a wife, and he'd outlive his kids.

"Oh, Dad. I'm so sorry you had to come back."

"It's not your fault, kiddo. Besides, it was an excuse to come see you." He released her, his deep blue eyes sweeping over her face. His bittersweet smile told her that he didn't miss how she'd aged from the eighteen-year-old he last saw, and it made him both proud and miserable. "It was bound to happen. I'm just glad... We seem to have a chance. To get everyone to listen and not live in fear anymore."

She nodded as she looked over his shoulder at Millie. The female hesitantly held her arms out, like she was never sure how she'd be accepted. Patience untangled from Dad and embraced her not-quite-stepmother.

Millie had been more like an older sister than a mother figure. Patience had been too young to remember her more than running and playing through the yard and following her to help with chores. Then they'd had to leave. During their last visit, they caught up on life, but neither of them could share much, mostly because there hadn't been much going on.

But Patience liked Millie. Clearly, she loved Dad. She had a good heart and a killer strawberry-rhubarb pie recipe.

"How are you doing?" Millie asked in her rich voice that Patience always envied.

That she admired her was an understatement. Millie was the first shifter that Patience could recall meeting. Brenden and Delia had been friendly but kept plenty of personal distance until Patience was older and they started working cases together. But Millie had come into her life, tall and gorgeous and kind. She was quick to smile, but when she thought no one was paying attention, there was always a hint of sadness, a stark tang of loss.

Millie spoke about leaving loved ones behind and that it was necessary, and it helped Patience and Jacob understand when Millie and Dad had to leave town for good.

"I'm good," Patience responded. "Really, really good."

And she was. Malcolm wasn't just her guest anymore; he felt like a partner. They still hadn't known each other very long, but when he confessed that no one knew him better than her, she felt the same. Jacob was her brother, but they didn't talk like friends. They didn't even really share their feelings or what happened to them in the past. It was all too secret. But she could share everything with Malcolm.

The corners of Millie's soft brown eyes crinkled. "Good to hear. We've been worried. I know Jacob told us that this shifter is fair, but..." She shrugged. "He's a Guardian."

"And he's staying here?" Dad's disapproving tone made Patience's lips twitch. He'd had to give up much of his role in her life, but he couldn't help himself.

"He is. And he's really a good guy. If anyone were to find out about you two, I'm glad it was him." Stepping back, she eyed their old pickup parked next to hers. Were they planning on staying here or camping out in the woods? "Come on, come in. Do you need a place to stay?"

She stepped inside and held the door open.

Dad ushered Millie in. "No, we won't be a bother. We brought a tent and a—"

Millie stopped and he bumped into her back. Both Patience and Dad stared at the suddenly pale shifter.

"What's..." Millie's brow crinkled and she inhaled. A

tremor shook her strong shoulders. "What's the Guardian's name? Who is it?"

"Who? Malcolm? I think his last name is Wallace."

Millie's eyes drifted shut. "Sweet Mother Earth. Why didn't I think of the possibility?"

"Sweetheart?" Dad put his hand on Millie's back and rubbed.

The details started to click in Patience's mind. Millie knew Malcolm. And that it was Malcolm here wasn't a good thing for her.

"He'll be back shortly." Just then, they heard his pickup. Malcolm approached, his pickup lumbering down the driveway.

"There he is. It'll be all right, Millie." Without knowing the story between them, there wasn't much more she could say.

Millie's mouth hung open, her stricken gaze on the pickup.

They all watched Malcolm step out and shut his pickup door as he evaluated the vehicle Dad and Millie arrived in. Then he was up the stairs, his gaze on hers before he opened the screen door.

Then just like Millie, he stopped as if he'd just hit a wall. His gaze swept over them, his chest inflating on an inhale. Then his gaze landed on Millie and he reeled back, letting the screen door go.

Millie's fingers twisted and she stepped forward. "Malcolm."

Patience rushed out after him. "What's wrong?"

Comprehension fused with deep betrayal in his eyes as he stared at her. "Did you know?"

"Know what?" She tried to get closer, but he was backing up, his pace steady and unfaltering as he took the stairs backward, shaking his head. "Malcolm, this is my dad and his mate, Millie."

His tortured eyes met Millie's. "Camille."

Oh. She understood now. Oh, no. Millie hadn't really changed her name, just dropped the beginning. A nickname of sorts. Enough to keep a connection from being made, like they advised her to do. To say Malcolm looked shocked was a gross understatement. This was the sister he searched so long for. The sister he thought he failed. The sister he was convinced had died alone in the forest.

Patience reached for him. "It's okay, Malcolm. We can talk about this."

It was the wrong thing to say. To his ears, she sounded guilty as hell. He must think she lied to him about this, too.

He shook his head and turned his back.

Millie appeared beside her, her shock subsiding enough to get her to move. "Malcolm. We need to talk."

But he ignored her, ignored them all. He got back behind the wheel, gunned the engine, and peeled away, not looking back.

HE DROVE. He drove, and he drove, and he drove. He used up the spare gas can and had to stop and fill his tank, but he hopped back in and kept going.

He hadn't registered where he was headed until he pulled up outside a square garage that sat adjacent to a tiny little cottage, a place where his past had reared up and interfered with his future.

At least it had seemed so. But that's what really happened today.

Camille. Millie. His sister. Alive and well and apparently mated to Patience's father.

How could she?

He didn't know which "she" he referred to.

As he slammed the door, he fixated on the two females who shattered his world. His sister had run away. Run away from her life, from her pack, from them. He and Harrison had nearly destroyed themselves searching for her and she had run away.

And Patience. Had she known? He couldn't think clearly, couldn't recall her reaction on the porch. The shock of Camille had slammed him back into the past.

He muttered to himself, asking the same questions over and over—Had Patience known who Millie was? Had she figured it out and not said anything? Was Camille that miserable?—as he stomped up the stairs to the door.

Harrison flung the door open and leaned against the frame. His dark eyes glittered over Malcolm. A smartass remark might've been on Harrison's lips, but the look he gave him now was full of questions and concern.

Harrison didn't bother to ask what was going on. Malcolm stopped at the top stair and faced him. It never felt like gazing into a mirror when he looked at Harrison. His brother had been the brooding one, had a darker edge. That wasn't true anymore, and that made them even more different at the moment. Harrison was relaxed, his expression no longer looking like he wished he was murdering someone, and sometimes he even cracked a joke.

Malcolm hated to take that away from him. "Camille's alive," he blurted.

Harrison sucked in a breath and stuffed a hand in the pocket of his jeans. Malcolm caught movement behind his brother. Sylva tucked herself into Harrison's side. His brother automatically put an arm around her.

She took Harrison's cue and didn't say a word either.

The story spilled out. "I met someone. Patience. She's human. And nice. Gentle. Mom would fucking hate her. And

169

she's the one working at that place I told you about, and she wouldn't tell me the truth but she didn't lie, and I didn't put two and two together, about how she helped shifters escape their packs and they change their names and shit and then she mentioned that her dad met a female through the center and her name was Millie and I saw her today. It's Camille. They both fucking...they just fucking..." He tried to say lied, but neither Millie or Patience had lied. He ground his teeth together. "So, yeah. Camille's alive and she's basically Patience's stepmother."

Sylva blinked, her violet gaze darting between him and up to Harrison. His brother's brow furrowed as he worked over the story.

Finally, Harrison pushed off the door but kept his arm around Sylva. "I'll pack a bag."

"I should go, too," Sylva said.

"In an official capacity?" Malcolm asked. Because he couldn't help but be the protective older brother and...whatever he was to Patience.

Patience's wide blue eyes flashed through his mind. She'd been floored at the revelation.

No one could've been more surprised than him, but she'd been shocked, too. That didn't quell the hurt kindling in his chest. Neither did it stop him from wanting to sink into Patience's arms, for only a few minutes, as he put his head back in order.

Harrison was the next best thing. His brother had to know, and Malcolm sure wasn't facing his mother without hearing Camille's story. Which he had to go back and do. He had a big job to return to, but he needed his partner, his brother.

He also wanted Patience. Seeing Sylva offer silent support to Harrison only highlighted what Malcolm had been missing. What drew him to Patience, other than her soft body and sharp mind, and her generosity and the way she just listened and joked around with him, like they'd known each other for years.

Sylva interrupted his thoughts. "I think it needs to be in an official capacity, but first, it's personal."

His brother and Sylva disappeared inside. Malcolm stuffed his hands into his pockets and paced on the small porch.

He didn't have much time to let his mind circulate over and over the same details. It was only minutes before the two were back out and locking up the door.

Harrison lifted his mate's bag and slung it over his shoulder. Without talking, they all went to the pickup. Malcolm crawled behind the wheel. Sylva gestured to Harrison to take the passenger seat and she got into the back, her phone to her ear, probably making arrangements with the Synod. He trusted her not to mention the specifics of finding Camille just yet, so he concentrated on getting them back to Patience —to Twin Forks. A portion of his coiled tension eased once he was heading in the direction of the little town.

"Wanna talk about Patience?" Harrison said quietly enough that they wouldn't be heard by whomever Sylva was talking to. "Is it that serious that you would actually tell Maw?"

Malcolm blew out a breath. "I...don't know." Patience wasn't some dirty secret. They were on opposite sides of a major case he'd fallen into working on, but in reality, they were on the same side. He wanted the best for his people and sometimes that meant going against long traditions and established laws that had worked for them for centuries but were oppressive during modern times. "It's not *telling* Maw. It's exposing Patience to Maw."

Harrison grunted. "I love Maw and all, but she's difficult."

"Yeah. I think that's our father's motto when it comes to

her. She hates humans and she has the exact mentality of the shifters that Patience helps others run from."

"Preserve our ways at all costs is no longer an option." His brother folded his arms and leaned his head back.

Malcolm pushed the speed as much as possible to carve as many minutes as possible off this trip. He'd been gone close to three hours. The pull to get back was getting stronger and stronger. He massaged the middle of his chest while keeping one hand on the wheel to maneuver the winding roads.

Harrison cut a sharp look toward him. "What's wrong?"

"Nothing. I just need to get back."

Maybe it was because they were twins, but Malcolm could tell that Harrison and Sylva were communicating without looking at them.

"What?" It's not like they had secrets.

"You feel like you gotta get back to your woman. Maybe you should call her."

His first instinct was to scoff. "I doubt anything's wrong. I left her with her father and Camille. I doubt our sister has gotten weak over the years." Over the *decades*. "Besides, we're just sleeping together. We've only known each other a few weeks." A sour taste filled his mouth. He and Patience weren't just anything. So why was it hard to admit that out loud and to his brother?

Harrison snorted. "Well, there are three of us in this pickup that can smell the lie."

"She's human, Harrison."

"I could name all the shifters we know with human mates. Aside from our own sister, there's Jace, his mama Armana, and—"

"In case you didn't hear," he liked it better when Harrison was a jackass that just let things go, "it's been three weeks. Humans with their short lifespans usually date longer before they decide to get married."

"Three weeks in a relationship is like three years for you." Malcolm gave his brother a sidelong glance, but Harrison shrugged. "Think about it. When have you thought about a female for three seconds after fucking them? For that matter, how much effort did you put into nailing them down?"

Harrison knew the answer since he'd been there with him for 99.9 percent of it.

"She found you in a ditch," Harrison said and Malcolm winced at the reminder. Not his finest moment. "You could've left the next morning, but you didn't." He held up his hand as Malcolm opened his mouth. "Don't give me the excuse that it was work-related. For the last how many months, have you stopped your sabbatical to work? Because I'm sure you saw a few things that would've justified it."

He didn't bother to reply. Sylva might be pretending to stare out the window to give them some semblance of privacy, but they all knew the answer.

"I won't even bother to ask how long you waited before you slept with her, or before she let you. If it wasn't the same minute you woke up, then she's broken the record of every other female you've been with." Harrison gestured to the pocket his phone was in. "Call her."

He didn't recall agreeing to Harrison's order when his phone was to his ear and her number was punched. It rang and rang.

"Shit." He tried again. "I'm sure she's just busy with her dad and our sister."

Neither one of his passengers commented as he pressed the gas down as far as it'd go.

CHAPTER 14

*P*atience pulled up to New Horizons. After Malcolm's sudden departure, she'd spent several stunned moments staring after him with Millie.

Camille.

Then Millie had looked at her, really looked, and Patience didn't have to verify whether she'd figured everything out. That her sort-of-stepdaughter and her brother were sleeping together, and from the sympathetic look in her golden eyes, Millie had deduced the depth of Patience's feelings for the male who stormed away like he'd never put Twin Forks in his headlights again.

Patience hadn't even confronted her own feelings. But he was so much more than anything she thought she'd have in life. All those failed dates. A stalker. Years of never really being seen and even longer of being alone. He'd wiped all those out with his first blistering kiss.

But several minutes ago, her phone rang, Rainey's ID popped up, and then it stopped as soon as it started. Patience had tried returning the call, but Rainey hadn't picked up. Then she'd tried Jacob because he was supposed to stay at the center until they found a place for Rainey. Since Millie—and subsequently, Dad—had the shock of their lives, she just told them that she was needed to help their new client.

Neither one could accompany her since Dad was supposed to be dead and Millie hadn't aged for the last couple of decades. Not that that stopped Tamera, but she was a different case altogether.

She should despise Tamera for telling Malcolm nearly everything so many people had tried to hide for years. But until a few hours ago, it seemed like there might be a promising turnout. Until Malcolm stomped away.

She didn't want to think that he was the type to turn vindictive and retract his support just because he was pissed at both her and his sister. But she hadn't seen this side of him, and from the way Millie spoke about their mother, she worried. Would he tell his Maw about her? Would he force Millie to go back to her colony and the pack and the male she was supposed to mate all those years ago if the Synod told him to?

Had he known about the plan to force Millie to mate?

Mostly, she worried that he would be poisoned into thinking she was nothing but a good time because she was human. And wasn't that selfish compared to what everyone else could be facing?

Patience got out of her car and eyed the building. A tendril of unease curled through her subconscious. The center didn't look any different. Having a shifter refugee under the roof always made her paranoid, but this was different. It felt like the place had a dark warning cloud hanging over it and she couldn't read what it said.

Scanning the street, she walked up to the back door. Cocking her head, she studied it. There was something different.

Just as she reached the path leading from the parking lot

to the door, a burly male banged it open. Like hers after Travis's intrusion, the door hung on one hinge. The slight crookedness it had retained after being shut was her only warning.

The male flashed her a wicked grin. He took in the shocked look on her face and the keys dangling in her hand. Add in that he was blocking the employee entrance she was about to enter and it wouldn't be hard for him to figure out she worked here.

"Well, it looks like I have myself my very own little bargaining chip."

Patience backpedaled, taking smooth, measured steps away from the back door. Were Jacob and Rainey okay? Who was this guy?

Her back hit a hard body. She cut off the yelp in her throat and spun around. Another large man was glaring at her, a calculating twist on his lips.

He clamped his hands on her shoulders. She boosted her knee straight to his crotch, but he easily deflected it. And from the looks of him, it might not have bothered him anyway.

"Now, now. I know you don't want to draw attention to us and that little bitch in the building."

Fear choked off her reply. These guys were shifters. And they came for Rainey. Even worse, he was right. Calling the police or doing something that could make someone else call the police would only end badly for all of them.

Too bad Malcolm had left.

The first one she encountered spoke disturbingly close to her ear. "We have ourselves a little standoff inside, and I'm guessing from all the salt in your break room cupboards that the human who thinks he can hold us off really does have a shotgun full of silver."

Yep. They kept one at the clinic, too. Jacob and Rainey

must've hidden as soon as these two showed up. They'd never had an incident, but Dad had made sure they were ready for one.

"So," he continued, nodding as he read the expression she couldn't hide well enough from him, "we'll see if you're worth trading."

The second shifter clamped his hand around her arm so hard her fingers went instantly numb and he dragged her toward the door.

"What's your name, sugar?"

She preferred Rescue Rabbit to the way he said sugar. It was no use fighting him. He'd want to prove her identity to Jacob and if she didn't do it for him, he'd do it the hard way. "Patience."

They hauled her inside and dragged her down the hall to the closed door of their guest room. Where Rainey and Jacob must be.

A female waited in front of the door, her arms crossed like a Centurion. She glanced over her shoulder and her bright green eyes flashed hateful fire.

"Another fucking human," she sneered and turned her attention back to the panel of wood. "Don't tell me that you thought humans could help you, Rainey? And you think I should trust you to make your own decisions?"

"It's my life, Mother," resonated from inside the room, trembling from anger or terror or both. "It's my right to find my mate in my own time."

The mother planted her hands on her hips. "You would've been fine with Sam here. Instead, you put two humans in danger."

Patience chanced a look from the corner of her eye at one of the males, then to the other. Which one was Sam? Considering they were willing to take a prisoner to force Rainey out of hiding, Patience didn't think that Rainey would've been fine.

"Wh-who's the second one?" Rainey sounded like she hoped she could call her mother's bluff, but knew better.

"Patience," the first male growled.

Neither Rainey or Jacob replied. What could they say? Obviously, she wasn't going to be let go just because one of them demanded it. They couldn't beg them not to hurt her, because these three new arrivals would totally hurt her if they thought it'd help. They needed time to think, but from the way the mother's fingers were tapping on her hips, time was dwindling.

"Rainey," she barked. "Open the damn door and we won't kill them. But for each minute you make me wait, we're tearing one limb off this weak little lamb."

She couldn't stop the tremble that shook her in their grip. She wanted Rainey safe, and she didn't want Jacob to do as he was told. But she also didn't want to suffer and die. But at least her pain would be quick before she either passed out or died. Rainey would be no better than a chained animal if they took her.

The door whipped open. With the shotgun in one hand, Jacob tried to block Rainey, but she gracefully sidestepped him. "Let them both go. Let them leave this building and drive away, then I'll go with you."

Patience shook her head, the same as Jacob. There had to be a way to help Rainey, but these three hadn't done much to her other than drag her through the center and she'd been powerless against that. Any more of a show of force and she and Jacob would be done.

The mother crossed her arms again. "You know we can't let them just go without wiping their minds."

Rainey paled, and the touch Jacob gave her was too familiar for the liking of the shifters. A low growl came from the one that must be Sam. Jacob slid a dark look toward him, as if to say it's the lady's choice, but he lifted his hand off her shoulder.

Rainey kicked her chin up. "Everyone knows about them, and they know about everyone. You can trust their discretion. I'm going back with you willingly." She turned her pleading gaze toward the male that didn't growl. "Let them go, Pa. Please?"

The two males both looked the same age, but they could be anywhere from thirty to three hundred.

Pa scowled, his brows dropping heavy with disapproval. "Not with some Guardian poking around. The way the Synod has gone soft, they're going to take a human's word over ours." He punched his dark gaze to Jacob. "You put down that shotgun and we'll go easy on you both."

Jacob's gaze sought hers. She clenched her jaw and tried to look strong for him. She didn't want to lose her memories, and she didn't trust that they'd do it easy. But she had the strength of a gnat against them.

It was her memories or Rainey's life. At least this way, she and Jacob would come out of it alive and that was easier to move on from than death.

The thunk of the shotgun against the wall rang ominously between them. Jacob's forehead was creased and he murmured to Rainey. She gazed at him as if she cared about him, as if she liked him more than a guy who was helping her through a bad time.

How much difference a few days made.

Envy bloomed inside of her. Would she recall her time with Malcolm after Pa and Sam were done with her? She might not, and then what? No goodbye. He left thinking she betrayed him, and while he might come to the realization that she hadn't, that was how things ended. With him walking away and never looking back.

179

She swallowed hard as Pa shoved her toward the mother. She didn't even know the names of the shifters who were stealing her precious memories. Mother, Pa, and Sam. She'd remember them. She'd have to. She couldn't just let them win, to steal Rainey away and ruin three lives while they did it.

Remember. Her pleas faded as she was caught in the mother's mesmerizing gaze. Jacob's voice faded, along with Rainey's protests.

The last thing flitting through her thoughts was Malcolm's stern profile as he drove away, her last view of him.

MALCOLM DIDN'T BOTHER to go to Patience's place first. Once they hit the edge of Twin Forks, he beelined for New Horizon. Harrison and Sylva stayed quiet. All they knew was that Patience lived out of town and they weren't heading out of town. He appreciated that they trusted he had a reason. He wasn't in an explaining mood.

The mild case of heartburn he'd had since picking Harrison and Sylva up turned into an inferno that burned through his chest and gut like he was nothing but a wick.

The intensity amplified when he skidded to a stop at the back of the center. Patience's car was here, and if he was drawn here so strongly, then the sick feeling that dogged him the whole way wasn't for nothing.

He hopped out, not bothering to kill the engine. It died behind him, probably thanks to Harrison.

Malcolm stalked to the door, his lip curling up when the scent of unfamiliar shifters wafted across his nose. Slowing, he approached the back entrance from the side. The sun was setting and hiding him from any curious onlookers.

There were no police. No other unfamiliar cars. The scent of other shifters was fading. They were gone.

Clicking open the door, he scrutinized it as it opened. Something was off.

There. By the hinge. Worn bits of wood still hung by a hinge that must've been recently busted. Whoever had been at the center wanted to make it look like they were never here.

Stepping inside, he peered around the quiet center. No one moved. Yet, Jacob and Patience's scents were strong and not lingering like they would if they'd gone home for the day.

Why had she come back? She left her dad and Millie at her place to come here. Had Jacob run into trouble. Was she baited?

He needed answers.

He sensed his brother behind him, but Malcolm was too busy following the smell of meadow flowers in full bloom. It led him straight to the room they kept for overnight clients.

Patience was curled on her side, one hand propped under her cheek and the other resting on her side.

Harrison stepped in behind him. "Sylva found a man asleep at his desk. Human." Harrison lifted his chin. "Her brother? They resemble each other."

Malcolm nodded once, his gaze cataloging the wrongness of this scene. "Jacob. There was a client staying here, a shifter. She's gone and so is all her stuff." Rainey's scent was fading but she'd been here at some point today.

Harrison ran his hand over the door frame. "This took a beating recently but held strong."

He went to Patience's side, worried the same happened to her, but she dosed, peaceful.

He tilted his head. "This isn't how she sleeps."

"Oh, yeah?" Harrison came to stand by him.

Malcolm nodded. "She sprawls across the bed and everything in it. Even the cats don't sleep with her for long. This is posed." What did it mean?

Harrison stepped back, not making a sound. "I'll hang out with Sylva until the brother wakes."

The privacy was necessary. Finding her didn't abate the dread raging through his gut. Something was still wrong. She looked physically okay, but something was wrong.

He swept his gaze over her. Black leggings and a baggy sweater. She wore the same outfit he left her in. He couldn't call her dad or his sister to find out why she came here. He had no way to reach them and Patience had said she didn't, either. There was no time to run to her place and ask them.

Fuck.

Stuffing a hand through his hair, he knelt by the bed. What happened?

She'd found him like this, curled on his side in a ditch full of dried grass, and shadowed by towering trees. She'd found him and helped him. It was his turn now.

"Patience?" he whispered. "Wake up, bunny."

She twitched, her mouth twisting in a grimace. She was in pain, but he couldn't see where. Had they beaten her and left her face alone?

"Patience?" he said a little louder and laid his hand on her shoulder.

Her eyelids flew open and she gasped. When her brilliant blue gaze landed on him, she let out a strangled scream and slammed herself against the wall and as far away from him as possible.

"Patience, hey. It's okay. It's just me."

She blinked, her gaze darting to the door and back. He might be able to tell Harrison waited out of sight after hearing her scream, but she wouldn't know.

She swung her wary gaze back to him.

"It's me. You're safe."

Her expression twisted into horrified confusion and she looked around like she was trying to figure out how she got here. Then she cowered back and met his eyes. "Who are you?"

His earth tilted on its axis and skidded to a stop.

What the ever-loving fuck?

"Malcolm," he said, feeling stupid that he had to introduce himself. He deserved it after the way he left, but he didn't get the feeling she was retaliating. He peered harder into the blue depths of her eyes, seeking some sort of recognition.

She blinked and somehow pressed herself harder against the wood paneling of the room, shrinking away from him.

She had no fucking clue who he was.

There was only one way she could lose her memory without a knock to the head.

"You don't remember me." He couldn't accept it. This had to be a sick joke.

She shook her head, panic rolling off her in a tidal wave.

He slowly put his hands up and backed away, staying on his knees. "I'm sorry. I didn't mean to startle you."

Her anxiety eased only slightly, and she sat straighter. "Who…" She licked her lips and pressed her fingers to her temples.

If she had a raging headache, then a significant amount of her brain was tampered with.

He had to work to keep from baring his teeth and growling. No more scaring her. But he'd kill whoever did this.

Disconnecting his logical brain from his emotions so he could function without terrifying her, he thought of how he should handle this. He couldn't remind her who he was to her, she obviously had no clue. He also couldn't explain what he was doing here because whoever did this probably wiped all of her shifter memories.

They might've done even worse if they came for Rainey.

183

But Patience was still alive, and he didn't plan on going anywhere. He'd committed himself to this little human and he'd make sure he left her better off—as she'd done for him.

Yet, his heart cracked at the thought that once he'd done that, they were done. He couldn't stay with her if she didn't know about his kind. It wasn't like they were true mates and he could just claim her and take his time. He wouldn't do that, and he couldn't risk being rejected and tampering with her memories again.

A brain could only take so much.

He kept his hands where she could see them and spoke softly. "I'm Malcolm, and I thought there was someone hurt in here. I wanted to make sure you were okay." She didn't relax, but her wan expression eased slightly. He hated her glassy eyes and hoped they could find some painkillers in the break room. But he had to find out what she did know. "Is there anyone else in the place with you? A friend or coworker?" A brother.

She scanned the room again. "Coworker?"

"My brother is here. Don't be alarmed if you see another me—we're twins. And his ma—wife is here too. They're making sure the place is safe and that you're not in trouble."

Massaging her forehead, she echoed, "Trouble?"

He thought of making up some lie, like they found the door open and a car speeding away, but he kept it simple for now. Until he knew more. "Right. Are you hurt anywhere? Or are you in trouble? Are you alone?" When she didn't answer, he dropped his hands and leaned forward as far as he could without causing her to make an impression of herself in the paneling. "Patience?"

She jerked her head up, then blinked and squeezed her eyes shut, a small sob escaping. "Who...am I?"

CHAPTER 15

*I*f she thought the first guy she woke up to was scary, his twin was worse. But unlike the twin—Harrison—Malcolm didn't stay scary. He looked at her with too much concern, his gaze spilling over with heartbreak.

She was so bad off that a complete stranger pitied her down to the depths of his soul.

The woman with them was kind and didn't tower over her. She was imposing enough, but tempered herself, it seemed, for Patience's benefit.

Funny the things she noticed when she didn't know a damn thing. She had all her motor control. Malcolm made sure of it.

Touch your nose. Touch your toes. If I asked you to make toast, would you know how? Do you know what toast is?

She knew how to live, apparently, just not who she was, or anyone around her. The center they called New Horizons, the other guy they also found asleep, who looked as dazed and confused as she felt, all that was strange.

Malcolm, Harrison, and Sylva had taken her and the guy they called Jacob around the building, pointing out pictures and certificates that had what was supposedly their names. Malcolm seemed to know her and Jacob.

He said that Jacob was her brother.

So, that was weird. Even weirder—Jacob didn't know who the hell he was, either.

A big 'closed' sign now hung on New Horizons and she was riding back to what was apparently her home with Malcolm and Jacob. Sylva drove the vehicle they said belonged to her and Harrison had taken the one they said was Jacob's. They must be right. She and Jacob had the keys to each of their vehicles on them.

How did two people get afflicted with total amnesia? She wracked her brain. Carbon monoxide poisoning? She didn't know much about it, but since she and Jacob had fallen asleep, it made the most sense.

Until she looked up symptoms on her phone, and nope. Not a lick of sense.

Her head throbbed, but there were no lumps or bruises.

She worried the damage was inside. "Why aren't we going to the hospital again?"

Scenery flew by in the pickup. Unfamiliar houses and roads. It was like she never stepped foot in this town, but according to Malcolm, she'd been born and raised here.

"They can't help you. You don't have a concussion."

Since she doubted two people could get the exact same concussion at the same time, she let it go. Part of her didn't want to be separated from Malcolm. He'd become the all-knowing one, and the caring way he looked at her was soothing.

"Am I married?" She might as well ask. Being overly comfortable around a man she didn't remember didn't mean there wasn't another.

"Ah, no."

Oh. The answer seemed…right. "How old am I?"

"Thirty-two."

"And me?" Jacob asked.

"Thirty-seven, I think."

Jacob drew his brows together. "How come you know her exact age but not—" She watched his gaze dart between them from the back seat. "Oh. Never mind."

Wait. Did he think... She looked at Malcolm. "Are you and I an item?"

This guy? This big and muscular man who had a mouth-watering body and looked like a woman would want to do nothing more than scale him and hold on tight for eternity. This guy, and her?

She'd looked at herself in the mirror before they left the center, the one time Malcolm let her out of his sight. Features so achingly familiar and strange at the same time. She looked at her reflection and thought *that's me* while at the same time going *who are you?*

But something in her brain gave her reason to think that they didn't fit the stereotype of a perfect couple. He was tall and broad and looked like he could leap tall buildings in a single bound. She hadn't tried to leap, but she looked like she could crochet a potholder and decimate a package of coconut macaroons in a single sitting.

Her cheeks burned even asking the question.

"Yes, Patience. We were."

Were. "Like, recently?"

His lips lifted at her incredulous question, but sadness emanated off him. "Yes, recently."

"What happened?" She felt like she was prying, but dammit, this was supposedly her life, too.

"We just don't work together anymore."

Her throat constricted and she fought hot tears burning the backs of her eyes. Something deep inside told her that it

187

wasn't the whole story, but his voice rang with too much truth to argue it.

Jacob leaned forward. "What about me?"

"Single, as far as I know."

Her brother sank back. "Figures."

"So, at your house is your—" Malcolm's expression crunched like he was doing timed calculus in his head. "Um, my sister and her...husband."

"But I thought we were broken up?"

"Recently."

She was going to her house, full of people she didn't know. What was his sister doing at her place? What was the reason for the breakup?

Malcolm took them through several turns and down roads that wound through trees. She lived pretty far out of town.

Then the trees cleared enough to reveal a cute little property with an aging but well-cared for barn, and weathered chicken coop and a cute two-story house with a detached garage. Two people waited on the porch, their solemn gazes watching the parade of cars entering.

Malcolm stopped in front of the far door of the garage. Sylva parked behind the closer door, and Harrison pulled in behind her.

"Wait here," he said. He didn't bother to see if she'd listen. He hopped out, slammed the door, and met up with Harrison. Sylva stayed in the vehicle, tossing a tense smile her way.

Something about this meeting seemed momentous, but it was her place. His sister. So maybe that was it?

Why did they break up?

Two dogs, one with only three legs, wagged their tails at Malcolm and gave his twin a thorough sniffing. They hovered over the brothers but didn't mow them down.

Her dogs?

Cats lazed in the shadows, watching their goings-on with a feline aloofness.

Her cats?

She and Jacob watched the twins approach the porch and speak to the tall woman with long, rich brown hair. She had it back in a braid and wore simple jeans and a T-shirt. The man on the porch had sandy blond hair and looked like he was only a few years older than Jacob.

Actually, he looked a lot like Jacob.

What was going on?

The female went from rigid to horrified, her hands going to her mouth. The man shook his head, his expression full of disbelief, and when he glanced toward her and Jacob, deep remorse.

"I feel like we're missing out on a lot of information," she said. They were siblings. She might as well confide in him.

"Yeah. I get that feeling, too. I also feel like they know exactly what happened, but that it's not their fault."

"Yeah. I guess that's why I'm still here and not running for the police."

"Ditto. I don't know much, but I know it's weird."

The woman looked so distraught, Patience had to look away. "Look," she said to Jacob. "There are goats and chickens. Do you recognize any of it?"

"Nope." A long sigh came from the back seat.

"I hate that this happened to you, but it's kind of comforting that we're in it together."

"Do you think we'll get our memories back?"

Did she? She'd been too busy trying to orient herself and make sense of the present that she hadn't thought of the future. "I don't know. How do you think they were...erased?"

"Chemicals? Some kind of medicine? That Vulcan move at the neck?" He laughed humorlessly. "I can remember that, but I can't recall what I do for a living."

She chuckled with him because she knew exactly how he felt. She could describe all the episodes she'd seen of *Outlander* and name how many days it took her to watch all the episodes of *Downton Abbey*, but she couldn't name that goat. Or those chickens that were supposedly hers. "It's the weirdest thing, isn't it?"

Definitely not natural. Like these people helping her and Jacob. Unnaturally keen, unnaturally gorgeous. Except for the guy on the porch with the twins and their sister. He had a sense of realness and she had no idea what it meant.

"They're coming back for us," Jacob said, his voice low. As if he had her back if she wanted to make a run for it. And in a way, she did. She wanted to run, but she wanted Malcolm to catch her.

Recently broken up. What had she done to get him to leave her? Or vice versa, but she couldn't imagine what it took to walk away from those muscles.

She let out a sigh. Was she this pathetic about him when she had her memory?

Malcolm opened her door. "You ready to go into your house?"

No. But she got out, hoping her body was full of muscle memory, because her brain was vacant. Jacob slid out behind her. Were they a family that held hands through hard times? Cracked jokes? Or just silently endured next to each other?

They had to be sort of close if they were both found in the center together.

Another door opened and closed. Sylva. She hung back and Harrison circled behind them to stay with her.

She followed the path from the garage to the house. The dogs ran up to her and she petted them, but without knowing their names or any-damn-thing else, she just let them be. The pavers were old and most were cracked. Had she put them in? If not her, who?

She briefly met the gaze of the two waiting on the porch, but she couldn't hold either one for long. The woman was distressed, twisting her hands, her lips flattened. And the remorse in the man's eyes welled over.

Malcolm's hand hovered at the small of her back and she wished he'd rest it there. She wished she could hide next to him and disappear.

"This is Camil—Millie." The emotion in his introduction couldn't be identified. "This is Millie and her husband, Paul."

Millie and Paul. Patience nodded at them, not bothering with handshakes. Seemed a little ridiculous in this case.

"So, um…" Patience gestured to the door. "You all have a place to stay?"

Millie shook her head. "Oh, don't worry about us."

"Were you staying here?" Patience asked.

"We'll find another place…"

"Why?"

Staggering regret lit Millie's gaze and she looked to Paul. His eyes were moist, like he was fighting back tears.

"It's just—" He cleared his throat, his gaze jumping from her to Jacob. "We stopped for a visit, but it turned out to be a bad time. We should…move on."

His 'move on' had a distinct ring of finality to it.

She had no idea what her personality was like, but right now, she was not emulating her name. Her patience was draining fast, being replaced with ire and irritation.

"No one's going anywhere. I don't know a damn thing and neither does he." She jerked her head toward her brother. "We don't even know each other. But every single one of you knows us and probably knows exactly what happened. This house must have more than one bedroom and at least one couch. So you're all staying."

With a huff, she yanked the door open and stormed inside with no idea where to go once she crossed the threshold.

~

THE SUN HAD SET hours ago. Patience was asleep in her bed.

Malcolm had only checked on her four or five times. Now he sat on the top step of the porch, a cat curled in his lap and two dogs snoring behind him. He went for a run every night. Every night she went to sleep, he had to run his wolf, run away from the heavy emotions, from the only conclusion that her loss of memory brought.

He'd have to leave her.

The front door creaked open and light footsteps stopped next to him. The achingly familiar smell of his sister reached him, but he didn't look up at her. They hadn't had much time to talk. The evenings had been filled with chores that Patience insisted on being a part of. Jacob too. They were only spectators, not remembering how to do a damn thing.

Why the massive memory wipe? Whoever had done it took a massive bulldozer and removed every part of Patience's life experiences. All but incredibly minor stuff, like pop culture.

Millie dropped next to him. She'd spent the last couple of hours in deep conversation with Harrison. Malcolm was more concerned about Patience. Millie had had decades to update him, after all.

"I'm sorry," she said.

He draped his arms over his knees, his hands hanging limp, barely moving enough to disrupt the cat. "Why?"

Her heavy breath got lost in the night-song of the local frogs and crickets. "My biggest regret was not telling you and Harrison what I planned. But with you both planning to be Guardians, I couldn't do that to you."

"You couldn't risk us stopping you, you mean." He wasn't usually so surly, but lies and incomplete truths had cost him too much over the days.

"That, too." She hugged her knees. "You two were going to get to leave Tame Peaks. I wasn't allowed to even find my own mate. Maw had me under her thumb and she fought with everyone. I was lonely, so isolated. And I was young enough to want a way out, no matter what."

"What happened to your horse?" She'd loved that horse. He couldn't believe she'd sacrifice it for her escape.

"Sold him. I needed money to re-establish my life."

She was desperate. That horse had been her best friend. The gravity of what her escape meant to her settled over him. "Would you change what you did?"

"No. I wouldn't change not telling you, either." When he gave her a sharp look, she shrugged. "Would you have done what you had to and turned me in? Made me go back home?"

He worked his jaw. It was his sister. But...he hadn't exactly been worried about being a progressive male. "I don't know. I would've helped you, though."

"And if you failed?" Her smile looked sad. "And you would've failed. These thirty years are short compared to our lifespans, but the last several years have been full of the most change our kind has seen. You would've done your job then, but I know you won't fail Patience now."

"I already did." She was scared. Hurting. And had lost so much. And she'd lose her dad, too. Paul Montgomery couldn't risk having human kids who knew about him and Millie. Their situation had completely changed.

"Not yet." For not having talked to him in so many years, Millie sounded like she had complete faith in his abilities. "When I fell in love with a human, I knew I could never be discovered. I could never go back home. If I got dragged back, Maw wouldn't allow me to be with Paul, and she'd gladly wipe his mind as fully as his children's were."

Everything she said resonated in a way it wouldn't have a month ago. Hell, not even twenty-four hours ago. Seeing someone who'd become important to him treated like she didn't matter? It was unacceptable. Maw's attitude was unacceptable. The lies and the hiding were unacceptable.

"I think Sylva will fight for us," Millie said quietly. "I think she's our biggest advantage."

"The other shifter on the board is honorable as well. He has a backbone."

"Unlike Father?"

"Father never cared enough to have a backbone."

"Harrison said he was well." She shook her head. "Our parents were forced to mate too, did you know that?" He jerked his gaze toward her. But she only nodded sagely. "More like contracted. But he found his true mate, a human, and they made him mate Maw earlier than planned."

Maw's resentment toward humans made more sense, along with her resentment toward everyone else.

"I was determined to have a better partnership than they did," Millie continued. "And for it to be at my own volition."

"And that happened."

"Yes. For Harrison and Sylva, too."

Malcolm nodded, numbness descending over him. He hadn't had a chance to find out if he could have a good partnership. He could get Patience through the worst of her memory loss, get her life back on track minus all things shifter, and then he'd have to move on.

"I have to talk to the neighbors about moving forward." About him leaving soon. He gazed across the dark yard. The chickens were nestled in their coop and the goats were in the barn. Nothing moved. "Tamera's there."

Millie jerked her head to stare at him, her eyes wide. "How's that been?"

"About as shocking as seeing you. Did you hear about Darius?"

"It was awful," she murmured. "I think she was actually happy with him, but I'm not surprised she survived his loss."

"We would've turned out just like Maw and Father."

Millie ducked her head. "I can't tell you how relieved I am to hear you admit that."

"Because she helped you." It wasn't a question. He'd had a lot of time to think on the drive to Harrison's and back, and his melancholy pondering out here on the porch.

"You know her ability, right? She can sense when two people are good together. That they're a match if there's no mating bond. Like our kind's divining rod if Mother Earth hasn't paired us with anyone yet."

"She mentioned it. How she knew she'd be okay with Darius."

"And how she knew that the male Maw wanted me to mate was wrong for me. I just knew my mate was out there. Somewhere."

He studied her. A profile that was achingly familiar but more mature than he remembered. More solemn. "Paul was your mate? Or just good enough?"

"No, I felt the pull to him, and the same with him. It was hard for him, though. He'd just lost a wife and wanted to do what was right for his kids. It only helped me trust what was between us more. I think he's what drew me here." She glanced at him. "You should question how you ended up in Twin Forks."

"I was looking for you. And here you are."

"Paul and I live deep in the woods, outside of another human town."

"Packless." Another problem waiting in the wings to be dealt with.

"Packless and with my wits about me, despite what they say. Think about it, Malcolm. I heard the story of how you were found."

Shame burned through him. She was his sister. Having her know how far off-track he'd been leveled them out. He was no longer the big brother who had failed her. He was just a brother who had his own messed-up shit to deal with, and she was sticking around to help.

"This was the likely outcome anyway. I just wish— It shouldn't have been so bad." But he'd force himself to go and not check up on her.

"You're not giving her a choice."

"What do you mean?" He didn't mean it to come out as crabby as it did. Neither of them had a choice, and like he'd said—it was inevitable.

"She hasn't lost her ability to make decisions. She hasn't lost her ability to choose for herself. You two were staying through all this together."

"I left her."

"I was there. I saw the way you looked at her. Yeah, you left to go tell Harrison about me, but you were also the first to find her. Paul and I would've been at home thinking she had a long case to deal with." Millie's breath hitched. "We might not have started worrying until late the next day. They would've been wandering around with no clue about anything. But you came back. Which is already way ahead of our parents."

"That doesn't mean she'll want to be stuck with me for eternity." The idea of being with Patience for years, stretching into decades, and moving into centuries, had a sense of rightness he couldn't describe. Being with Patience had always been like that.

"But it does mean that you two should make the decision together. I can't speak from experience since Paul knew about us, but most shifters have to face where you're at. Worrying about telling their human love about their kind and getting rejected." He opened his mouth to give the same argument that'd been replaying in his brain—that Patience no longer knew about him, that he couldn't know they were destined mates, that a second mind wipe could leave her with lasting damage—but his sister kept going. "We all know what's at stake for her, but don't be a chickenshit and walk away because it's easier."

Don't be a chickenshit. No one had called him that since she was ten and taunting him about how he'd run over Maw's rhubarb patch with the lawnmower and didn't want to tell her.

Should he stay or should he go? Millie's talk about letting Patience decide for herself was all well and good, but the problem was too complex to decide on in the dark on the front porch listening to regular wolves howl in the distance.

"I gotta talk to Brenden and Delia." He had to prepare for the inevitable. He gently dislodged the snoozing cat and handed it off to Millie. She looked like she needed to sit and contemplate life for a while. She accepted the bundle and the dogs shifted to sit beside her.

He strode through the yard, behind the house, and into the trees. The clouds parted enough to let moonlight through, but he'd have an easy enough time anyway. His skin crawled to go for a run. In such a short amount of time, he'd gotten dependent on his daily runs through the forest surrounding Patience's property.

After he talked to the neighbors, he'd go. He had a lot to think about, but mostly he had to move past what Camille said and do what was best for Patience, even if it felt like the wrong thing to do.

CHAPTER 16

*S*leep evaded Patience once again. She'd been snoozing until late in the morning the last few days. Jacob was staying in the house with her, in a bedroom in the basement. With the twins' help, he sent a message to the rest of the staff that he and Patience had a family emergency and had to leave town.

Harrison and Sylva were staying at one of the motels in Twin Forks while Paul and Millie were also in the basement —with a cat and six kittens that Patience had apparently rescued. That was her thing, they told her.

She was acutely aware that Malcolm slept on the couch.

That wasn't all he did.

He also turned into a goddamn wolf.

No one seemed to know that she'd seen him. The first night they'd brought her home, she couldn't sleep. So she gazed out the window from a little reading chair she'd moved there. But she hadn't turned on the light. The throb in her head hadn't gone away, so she was content to sit in the dark and let her mind wander. Who knew? It might stumble onto something.

Her mind didn't, but her eyes did.

She watched Malcolm disappear into the trees, and then an hour later, he came back, stripping his clothes off as he went. She followed him through the windows, tiptoeing through each room, grateful there was more than one floor between her and her guests, chastising herself for violating his privacy.

But he was undressing on her land. And his body was magnificent. The throb transitioned from her head to farther down in her body until she clenched her legs together as she spied on him. She'd been so painfully aware of him since she opened her eyes earlier, but this was different. So, so different. Her body knew what he could do to her even if her conscious mind forgot.

Peering out the bathroom window, she watched him disappear behind the garage. Only the land sloped upward, and with the hint of moonlight, she saw him drop his pile of clothing. What came next left her mouth hanging open, her headache roaring back, and her questioning her sanity after all.

His body dropped into a smooth transition. Supple skin flowed into a fur-covered hide over a damn big wolf.

She'd blinked. She rubbed her eyes. The wolf was gone.

So she'd waited, her eyes not leaving that mound of clothing no matter how her head ached.

Then the wolf came back, shook itself, and flowed back into a human. Nothing like TV. A natural process, so cohesive that she questioned what she really saw. In one second, there was a man where a wolf once stood. A stunningly naked man.

She rubbed her temples. Facing him while playing it cool had taxed her and her aching head. Between acetaminophen and ibuprofen, she'd made it through to each night for the last three nights where she watched the same thing happen.

That wasn't all she watched. Harrison and Millie were his siblings. Could they do the same thing? What about their spouses, Paul and Sylva? She hadn't seen any of them shift into anything else, but stayed the beautiful people they were.

But she'd noticed other things.

Harrison and Millie stopped talking to each other well before she was in the room, like they'd heard her coming from across the house. Sylva took her phone calls by the tree line, the same as Malcolm. That was more than out of earshot. And if they weren't on the phone, then Malcolm, Harrison, and Sylva were crowded around each other in a deep discussion by the farthest reaches of her yard. A discussion that stopped when Patience left the house.

She'd tried eavesdropping by an open window, but their murmurings weren't strong enough to drift on the wind more than a few feet away from them. How could they hear each other talking that low?

Paul was perceptive, but he didn't track her movements like the others. Even Sylva seemed to clock every action, like the cats when they were lying in wait in tall grasses for a mouse to make a move.

Or like a wolf hunting rabbits for lunch.

Nothing about them gave her a personal sense of danger. Instead, they surrounded her and Jacob like a protective ring.

But they were different. Jacob didn't stop talking before she entered a room. He didn't have any sense that she was about to sneeze, or lying about how badly her head hurt. He fumbled around the goats and dropped at least one egg a day when he tried to help with the chickens.

The others were different. Her main question was whether they were different like Malcolm.

Since Malcolm never made a sound when he left on his… whatever they were…she only knew to start watching depending on the time. He'd check on her and then go outside.

Was the reason for their breakup over his other side? Was she not supposed to know about his wolf? Or was it horrible that she didn't know?

There. Long strides carried Malcolm to a different spot tonight. He always varied his time, but her window was high enough to see beyond her squat barn and chicken coop.

He went through the same routine. Strip. Change. Run.

The rest of the house was quiet. She put on the fluffy pink robe that must've been her favorite and crept downstairs. The others were so attuned to noise and movement that she took extra time, gingerly setting her weight on each step. Her guests might be sleeping in the basement, but she was suspicious they could hear her if she didn't try. They might anyway.

Walking through the living room, she used the path that creaked the least. A week ago, she might've had a route that wouldn't out her, but she'd only had a couple of days to notice where the noisy spots were.

Slipping outside, she winced as the door creaked, but she finally reached the porch.

Now what?

She hadn't thought out whether she'd linger around his clothing pile and say "Surprise!" Or spy on him from another hidden place. Since she didn't think she could hide well enough to escape the notice of a supernatural wolf, she dropped to sit on the top step.

Cats flitted through the yard, but the dogs waited for Malcolm. They seemed to know his routine and were the main reason she wasn't terrified. If a three-legged dog got excited about Malcolm's nightly runs, then he couldn't be the type to rip innocent creatures apart, including her.

She had to have known this about him. If she discovered

his other side without half her memory, then they must've been honest with each other.

Her wait wasn't long. He circled around the barn, concern etched into his features.

"Are you all right?" His voice carried only far enough to reach her.

She couldn't do the same so she nodded and patted the seat beside her.

He paused a few feet away, his gaze riveted on the spot next to her. The troubled look in his eyes made her think that he was deciding if sitting next to her violated the way he physically and mentally distanced himself from her.

"I couldn't sleep," she whispered, barely pushing air beyond her lips. "I needed the quiet."

His gaze sharpened, but he sat, and the addicting scent of fresh pine with a touch of sweat curled around her like a security blanket. The smell teased the edges of her mind.

"Are the headaches back?" he asked.

"Yes." Since she'd first seen him transition to another species, yes. Her memories were banging against the cage they'd been trapped in.

"Did you take some medicine?"

"Every four to six hours," she said wryly. If she didn't remember, Malcolm was next to her with a glass of water and a palm held out with painkillers.

He didn't cater to Jacob like that. Jacob's head bothered him, but from the way he roamed the yard, his brows drawn in concentration, she suspected he was fighting his affliction and digging deep to recall anything about his past.

Malcolm shifted a few inches away from her, leaned his arm against the railing, and let out a long sigh. Those three inches turned into a yawning void, sucking away his body heat she marinated in. "Harrison and I were talking about leaving tomorrow."

She expected him to leave, but not quite so soon. "Why?"

"You can function fine, and maybe you can rebuild a normal life without our interference."

Did he think her headaches were worse because she was trying to remember him? Them? He'd be right, just not totally in the sense he thought. "What about Millie and Paul?"

Calling Millie's husband Paul was foreign on her tongue. Like his simple name wasn't right. Had she called him anything else?

So many questions.

He brushed his hand over his beard, the move causing an answering echo in her own palm. A tingly, silky sensation. "They're going to stay with you a little longer and make sure you get settled into work. Can I give you a tip?"

She gave him an expectant look.

"Don't let your coworkers walk all over you. If they keep calling in sick on you, just shut the center down for the night."

"I didn't before?"

He shook his head. "You'd work doubles, or stay overnight, even when it wasn't a—when it didn't have to be you."

That was a little cryptic. Some hidden meaning she might've known a few days ago.

She mulled over his announcement. He was leaving. Yet his shoulders hung as if he were being dragged away against his will. He'd been shadowing her for three days, not to mention that he was the one who rescued her in the first place. They used to be an item. And now he was leaving but couldn't help but pass along advice.

He cared about her, and it couldn't be more than her wishful thinking that it went deeper than friendship. She didn't care how a plain Jane like her snagged a bearded beast like him, but she had—and she wanted to keep him. Whatever brought them together was something special, and she wasn't going to ignore it.

To move past this memory thing, she needed answers that were currently locked in her brain.

She crossed her arms and scooted away from him to lean her back against the house. They were on opposite sides of the opening the stairs made, but she wanted to see his face when she asked her question.

"Okay, I'll keep that in mind. But before you go, I need to ask about Millie and Paul. Can they turn into a wolf like you?"

MALCOLM'S MOUTH WENT DRY. She didn't ask what he just heard? He had to be hallucinating. There was no way she could—

"Turn into a wolf?" he scoffed, but from the set expression she had, it was pointless. "What'd you see?"

An adorable blush, one he'd missed every excruciating night for the last four days, graced her cheeks. "Everything." She chuckled nervously. "I couldn't sleep the first night and was staring out the window."

"But I went behind the barn." She'd been watching him each night?

"The one window overlooks the whole yard and it slopes up into the trees so…" Her flush deepened.

He stared at her. She managed to discover his species' biggest secret in less than twenty-four hours after her mind was locked tight.

She'd grown up knowing about shifters. She'd grown up with one foot in their world and one foot in her own, but both areas mixed for her far too often. It was natural for her and taking it away was unnatural.

A surge of hope soared through him before he could stop it. She knew about him.

Did it change anything?

Her brows were pinched, but it wasn't concentration clouding her eyes. She had a headache, and he was probably the reason. Her mind was fighting its confines. The Synod had to consider that.

He'd make them. Because his ass was staying here. With her. He started by answering her question. "Millie shifts, but Paul is your dad."

She reared back, her head glancing off the Masonite siding of her house. "Paul is my dad?" Concentration infused her expression. "Father, Pa, Daddy, Dad. Dad. Dad, Dad, Dad, Dad." Her face brightened. "Dad. Yes, that feels better to say."

His lips quirked and a chuckle resounded into a laugh. "Sweet Mother Earth. You've rescued yourself."

The pinch of her brows eased. "Like the seven cats in the basement?"

"Like me when you dragged me from the ditch."

Her eyes went wide and distant, like she was searching for the memory. She pressed her fingers to her temples.

"Shh." He edged closer to her and eased his fingers over hers. "Don't push it. Just let me tell you everything and let your mind soak it in."

She dropped her hands and he took it one step further. Maybe more than one step. He nudged her around until she reclined against his chest and he lightly massaged her temples as he told her the story of how they met, up until this moment.

Several minutes went by after he stopped. Her breathing was soft, but she wasn't asleep.

"That's a helluva life," she finally said. "I bet I thought I was boring."

"You've never been boring."

"I'm sure after six hours straight of *Shameless* you'd think that maybe I was a little dull."

"Not even after the time you made me watch that British baking show for five hours."

"I never forced you to watch—" She jerked up and spun around to him. "We never watched that together, did we?"

They were coming back. "No. What else do you remember?"

She blinked and that crease between her brows returned. "It's all getting fuzzy again. Touch me some more."

Without the heaviness of her recent trauma, he wasn't sure he could touch her and prevent his body from being obnoxious. The thought of getting his hands on her again was already sending blood flowing south.

She leaned toward him, her eyes searching his and her hands braced on his knees. His body soaked up her touch. "If you were going to end things because of my memory loss, what happens if I get it back?"

"I... We go back to before. You can help us locate Rainey and we'll take everything to the Synod. They already know what's happened. Sylva has been keeping them informed with your neighbor's help."

More rapid blinking. "My neighbors are shifters?" Her hands moved to his chest, desire infusing her gaze. "What if we touch a lot more?"

He stilled. That she wanted to be with him again was a dream he thought had been snatched from him. But doing it like this, for this reason? "If I could fuck your memory back, that's not very fair to you. You can get it back without—"

"Malcolm, since I woke up to you at the center, my body has been informing me that you can do wicked things to me. I've wanted to be with you since then. I still want to be with you. It has nothing to do with my memory."

He'd wanted the same. Right now, they were just two

people who were drawn together and didn't care to fight it. He scanned the yard. "We can't do it in the house." With her dad and brother under the same roof? No way.

"My car."

"My truck," he said as he swooped her up in his arms. Long strides ate up the distance to his pickup. He opened the door and carefully set her inside. She scooted back far enough to let him in, but he took his time shutting the door.

Nearly four days of thinking it was over between them, he wasn't ruining the moment by waking everyone up with a door slam.

Once he was settled inside, they became a flurry of movement.

He did what he'd been trying not to fantasize about while he was hard as stone on the porch and alone each night. He pressed her back and loosened the knot of the robe at her waist. Then he dropped his head to the waistband of her pajama pants and dragged them off with his teeth.

Her meadow flower scent bloomed in the cab and he inhaled deeply. His fangs throbbed to claim her, but he wouldn't do that until she had full access to her mind and was shouting "Yes, do it" as he plunged in and out of her.

But that didn't mean he couldn't taste her. He spread her legs to make room for his shoulders and he didn't worry about whether she wanted him to or not. She made her desire perfectly clear. From the glistening folds waiting for him and her hands twisting in his hair and bringing him closer.

He dove in like a starving man, licking and nibbling her ready and sensitive flesh. It only took seconds before she was muffling her cries with both hands as she jerked under him. Her taste filled him, her scent was all over him, and the word ripped out of him. "Mine."

She pulled him up her body. "Yes. I do believe I am." She

caressed her fingers over his cheeks and down his beard. "And I think you're mine."

"Don't doubt it, Patience. I've tried to be reasonable about us. I've tried to think that this might not be real and lasting, but I can't. You've been different in every way, in all the important ways."

"We'll get through this. Together."

"Together," he agreed as he claimed her mouth. He didn't bother with his clothing, he just ripped open the fly of his jeans. Once his cock was freed of its confines, he shoved inside of her.

He swallowed her moan and pumped like a male who needed to orgasm to survive. And since he'd felt like an empty shell since she woke up not knowing who he was, that might just be the case.

Her body surrounded him, her tight walls fisting him tighter than he could ever remember. Every time with her was a new experience, showing him the depths this thing between them could go to if they only had a chance.

As fire laced up his spine and his climax hit him like a brick wall, he could only think that his goal in life was to make sure they had a chance.

CHAPTER 17

"*A*nd you were just curled up there? I almost drove by?" Patience was sprawled across Malcolm's chest. They'd righted their clothing but stayed snuggled in the back of the pickup. She was making sense of the information dump Malcolm gave her.

"I'm sure you did. You'd just pulled a twenty-four-hour shift."

"Why?"

He rubbed her back, content to hold her, just like she could stay in his arms forever. "You were helping someone. And I'm sure a coworker didn't show up."

"That happen often?"

"At least three times in as many weeks."

"I'm a pushover." To say it was weird hearing about herself was an understatement. But it *was* weird.

"You're a helper, don't ever be ashamed of that. If someone takes advantage of that, it's on them."

What would work be like? She and Jacob couldn't avoid it forever. They'd tossed around ideas, like some kind of illness that made them foggy on...everything. She'd eventually tabled the discussion until she was forced to figure something out.

Malcolm tensed and craned his head around to look out the window. She pushed off his chest to see what alerted him, but his tight grip around her held her down. After a moment, he eased enough to let her peek out the window.

Jacob was creeping across the sidewalk to his car. She only recognized him because he was shorter than the twins and she couldn't picture Paul—Dad—creeping. Knowing now what she did of everyone, she wanted to tell him it was useless. By the time he was up the stairs, Millie and Dad were probably right behind him.

"What the hell is he doing?" she asked.

"I guess we'd better find out."

Malcolm carefully righted them and set her on the truck seat before opening the door. "Evening, Jacob. Care to share where you're going and why it's such a secret?"

Her brother recoiled and looked around. He recovered and shifted from foot to foot, his gaze darting from them to his car. "I gotta go."

Malcolm slid out, an efficient move that was both predatory and non-threatening. "Where to, bud?"

Jacob scowled. When he moved, the moonlight reflected off his keys, his hand clenched around them. "Am I a prisoner?"

She had only really known Jacob for three days, but this was out of character for him. He was congenial, mellow, and in awe of the twins. At the moment, he was tense and looked ready to fight Malcolm if he kept delaying him.

"No, but it's the middle of the night and you don't remember anyone."

She climbed out behind Malcolm. She hoped Jacob couldn't see well enough to view her flaming blush. Being busted doing the deed in the back seat wasn't fun at any age.

Concern and curiosity took over. Where was he going in the middle of the night?

"What are you two doing in the back seat of—" Jacob's mouth snapped shut and he squinted at her in the dark. "I guess it's back on."

She crept forward. "I know we've been shut up here for days, but you and I are in this together. Want to tell me where you're going?"

Shadows nearly concealed his grimace. "I just have to go, I can feel it."

Malcolm cocked his head. "Feel what?"

Movement on the porch caught Patience's eye and she jumped. Her dad and Millie were watching Jacob. And likely saw her and Malcolm climb out of the pickup, too.

Jacob followed where her attention went. Instead of turning defeated, he ground his jaw and marched to the front door of his car. "I can't describe it. I need to go."

"Can you guys compel others?" she breathed to Malcolm, knowing Jacob wouldn't hear more than a sigh.

Millie lifted her brow at Malcolm. He shrugged and mouthed something she couldn't hear but was likely along the lines of *She figured it out.* Millie murmured to Dad and he nodded. Despite the shadows, relief crossed his face. The emotion was wiped out when he looked back at Jacob.

"Son," Dad said, "is it a something or a someone you're being drawn to."

Jacob's shoulders fell but he didn't remove his hand from the door handle. "All I keep thinking is, 'she needs me.'"

She?

"Does she have a name?" Malcolm's voice was steady and solemn.

"No. But I have to get to the center. Now." He opened the door and climbed in. Malcolm jumped in the passenger side.

Patience went to get into the back, but Malcolm poked

his head out the door. "Stay with your dad. I'll call Harrison and Sylva."

She nodded and hugged her robe around herself. She wouldn't be much use in her pajamas and flip flops.

Jacob backed out and gunned the car down the driveway.

Patience watched them go before addressing the couple at the base of the porch. "I've been watching Malcolm shift the last few nights and assumed you were all the same. He told me everything."

Dad crossed the distance between them. Millie hung back, giving them some privacy. "You were always an observant one."

"Is Jacob okay?"

"We don't know if he had any kind of connection with anyone."

She wouldn't know, either.

Dad's gaze trailed from her to the pickup, his mouth set like he wasn't sure what to think about the new development in either of his children. He didn't look or act much older than her, but he must be close to seventy. His white shirt stretched across his chest and he had on blue jeans. Millie was dressed as well. Both were ready to follow Jacob.

He was her dad. But he also hadn't raised her. Malcolm had described her grandmother. All the vehicles were sitting outside because the garage was full of her grandma's stuff. She'd lost them all. She wasn't losing Dad again, and she wasn't losing Jacob. Malcolm would make sure of it.

"Why don't you come inside?" Millie said gently. "Malcolm will let us know what's going on after he and Jacob are done at the center."

"I'm not tired." Between her hookup with Malcolm and Jacob's sudden leaving, her mind was whirring. "I might wander around the yard a bit."

Millie and Dad exchanged looks.

"I'll be fine," she said.

"But you won't mind if your old man waits on the porch?"

She gave him a small smile, warming at seeing the man she'd only been told was her dad acting like it. "I won't mind."

The shifters who wiped her mind didn't have anything more to do with her. They took what they wanted and she couldn't speak against them to the Synod, if that would've done any good in the first place.

She picked her way through the dried grass, trying to be quiet for no reason other than she didn't want to disturb the peaceful slumber of her animals.

She circled around the goat pen. The world behind the trees loomed dark and the hairs on her arms prickled. Skirting close to the building, she was about to round to the other side, when Tripod appeared in the opening of the barn inside the pen.

His low growl reverberated through the night. She froze. She couldn't see more than his outline in the dark. The dog had been nothing but loving and affectionate. If Tripod was growling, something was wrong.

She didn't dare risk a look toward the trees. Somehow, she got her feet moving again, faster than before, and much louder. Tripod wasn't barking, but his growls came in waves. She cleared the side of the barn, her heart beating so fast it was going to escape her ribcage, when she slammed into someone.

She opened her mouth, a startled scream ready to escape, when a hand clamped over her mouth.

"Shut it, Rescue Rabbit, or you're going to get gobbled up."

～

STREET LAMPS LIT up the sidewalk in front of the center and the security light by the employee entrance cast its glow over the door. Nice and ominous.

Malcolm gestured to the side of the road and said, "Park here," to Jacob.

"But—"

"You wouldn't be in such a rush if there wasn't something wrong." Malcolm wasn't so sure about that, but he doubted the man would be so compelled if someone left a box of thank you donuts on the doorstep.

It was enough for Jacob. He pulled over and killed the engine, but his gaze searched the surrounding area. Malcolm did the same, but he could see way better.

What had brought Jacob here?

He saw a flicker of movement in the bushes that bordered the yard and he zeroed in on it. After a few heartbeats, an outline of a body was visible.

A female. She crouched in the bushes, peering at the car as he watched her. Finally, she crept out and glanced around before jogging toward them.

She was tall with long, dark hair and she only had eyes for Jacob.

Rainey.

The reason why Jacob and Patience went through what they did. Was she the reason why Jacob was compelled here?

Why was she back in the first place?

It didn't bode well. Trouble was on her tail.

"That's her." Jacob sat straighter. "She's why I'm here."

There's no point in asking why. Jacob wouldn't remember.

"Stay in the car." Malcolm got out. Rainey stopped on the other side of the sidewalk, the boulevard yawning between them. "Wish you could've called first," he said dryly.

She didn't bother to look at him, her only attention was for Jacob. "Is he okay?"

"Why are you back?"

"I escaped and came for him. Is he okay?" she repeated, her gaze fraught.

"Neighborly concern is nice and all, but coming here endangered him more." A car door clicked open behind him. Dammit, Jacob. "If they touch his mind again, he could go insane."

"Was it bad?" She wrung her hands together. The pants she wore were too short for her tall frame and her T-shirt was a few sizes too small. She looked like she raided a teenage boy's closet. Considering that she probably ran here on foot, perhaps a little breaking-and-entering happened along the way.

"It is bad," he said. "They took all the memories of everyone in his life, including his own identity." She blanched, but she wasn't getting away that easy. "Why did you come back? And why was he drawn here?"

"You should be able to figure it out since you're the same about his sister." She wrung her hands and cast a pleading look toward Jacob. "I'm so sorry."

Before Malcolm could process what she said, Jacob came around the side of the car. "You're why my memory was taken."

She nodded. "We didn't know each other, but you and I... we're connected."

For fuck's sake. They were mates. This just got a lot more complicated. Jacob and Rainey were in the same position he and Patience had been in, but it wasn't like he could tell them to go fuck and talk it out. He doubted they'd built much of a relationship in the short week they'd had together.

Awareness prickled down his spine. "You were followed."

"No. I promise I wasn't." She didn't smell like she was

215

lying, but she also wasn't like him. She had shifter senses, not shifter senses honed from danger.

"You were, and this time, I doubt they sent only a few." He'd dealt with enough colonies like Rainey's. They didn't tolerate disobedience more than once before they did something radical. And they probably thought like his Maw. A dead human mate was better than a living one. He gestured to Jacob. "Get in the car."

"I'm not leaving him again."

What she didn't get was that she didn't leave him the first time—they dragged her away—and her people would gladly drag her away again. But Jacob was safer with her than alone. "Get in with him. And go ahead and tell him about us because I think he's going to see more than enough soon."

Where were they coming from?

Without any weapons, he'd do better in his wolf form, but they were in the middle of fucking town.

I'm here. Harrison's voice drifted through his mind. *Sylva's watching the front. There's a plain gray car driving through town and the guys inside don't look like they're playing around. They're looking for someone.*

That someone is in Jacob's car. They're mates.

Harrison didn't have an immediate reply, and it wasn't because he was relaying information to Sylva. Those two had a strong enough connection that Sylvia could listen in. *Why so many mates in Twin Forks? Odd, isn't it?*

What do you mean?

Millie and Paul. Jacob and this Rainey. You and Patience.

Patience isn't my mate. He couldn't even keep the bitterness out of his thoughts. Patience wasn't obligated to him, and she knew about them and their life, she figured him out. But none of that meant she was willing to spend hundreds of years together. Or willing to give up her home and her job to follow his sorry ass around.

A whole family of shifter mates, Harrison interrupted his brooding. *It's like you and Millie and Rainey were drawn here.*

They've helped a lot of shifters. It's a secret network of shifters helping shifters escape.

Sylva's voice broke through with a hint of exasperation. *What he's speculating about is that maybe it's nature at work. Patience and her family aren't a problem if they're mated to shifters.*

But then they can't help shifters.

Maybe they won't need to. The problem has been brought to the Synod's attention and you bet your ass we're going to deal with it and these backwoods packs who think they can live like it's the Middle Ages.

Malcolm smirked. Sylva wasn't heedlessly confident. She had to know what the Synod was thinking and which way they were all leaning. Things were going to change for his people.

Things were going to change for him. He'd already made the mistake thinking that his destiny was meant to be. Tamera chose her own destiny. If Patience was meant for him, regardless of mating instinct, she still got to choose.

A tendril of unease curled through his belly. Patience.

His body went rigid.

Patience.

Something's wrong. He went to Rainey's window. From the incredulous way Jacob stared at him, he gathered that she'd told him what they were. "Who could've followed you?"

"I ran here. On foot, like I did before. I followed the river, and before you say what a dumb idea that was, I didn't plan to stay long. I found Jacob and waited here for him. That was our plan. It was the only reason I let them take me in the first place."

"What do you mean you found him? How long have you been back in Twin Forks?"

"I arrived several hours ago. I went to his house. When he didn't show up, I found her address on his desk." She sounded defensive but worried she'd fucked up and risked her mate. "I waited until after dark. No one saw me."

Jacob had a week with the shifter and probably fell madly in love. She was distraught and he'd be drawn to her. "I'm not worried about humans seeing you. I'm worried about who followed you. And how they're going to use Patience to get you back."

CHAPTER 18

"*D*on't move." The woman's breath hissed across her ear. "I owe Malcolm, and saving your ass makes us even."

She didn't sound like a friend, and her punishing grip wasn't kind, but Patience clung to the *saving your ass* part. She nodded.

The woman dragged them both to the far edge of the barn. "I'm gonna get you back to the house where Millie can protect you."

What about Dad? Oh. He was human. "You're a shifter."

"Duh." She flipped hair that was probably blond in the daylight. "Oh wait. Like, you lost *all* of your memories?"

Patience nodded.

"Shit. But you smell like sex. Malcolm's still fucking you?"

How her personal life became so widely known, she'd never know. "I figured it out."

"Rescue Rabbit, sometimes you really surprise me." Tripod growled and Patience stiffened. The woman grabbed her hand. "They're closing in. Move as fast as you can and don't fucking fall."

The woman jerked her arm and Patience nearly tripped immediately, but she stayed upright. "What about the animals?"

"You can't rescue them if you're dead, and these shifters want to make you pay. Run."

They each broke out in a sprint. Patience concentrated on each step, debating whether to chuck her flip flops off and worrying that they'd trip her.

Her dad appeared next to her, keeping pace. "Tamera, thank God."

Tamera. Malcolm told her about Tamera.

Tamera saw her expression. "Don't read into it. I'm itching to fight these kinds of bastards."

Millie stepped out, a shotgun in her hand. She lifted her chin at Patience. "Take this and get inside. Anyone comes through the door that isn't one of us, shoot 'em."

"Unless it's Brenden or Delia," Tamera added. "Do you remember them?"

"No." She eyed the heavy weight of the gun in her hands. Could she point and shoot? A gun made sense in the country, but for rabid animals that wanted to bite her, not people.

Tamera shrugged. "Guess we'd better tell them to stay outside." She disappeared into the dark depths of her property, stripping her shirt off, Millie following behind.

Dad ushered her into the house. "I'm sorry, Patience."

She blinked at him. "This isn't your fault."

"My way of life robbed me of a life with you. I missed so many things. You were so little when I left and I kept telling myself that I was one of the lucky ones. Most human mates have to walk away from their families and never talk to them again." The corners of his eyes crinkled. "But seeing how much you've grown, the person you've become, I should've stayed. Millie and I would've figured something out."

"Regrets won't do us any good. We can only move

forward." She went to the couch and sat with the shotgun between her knees. Unknown shifters encroached on her place, presumably for her, and she couldn't do anything but sit here.

"You sound like your mother. She would've been so proud of you."

Regret coiled around her heart. "I hope I remember her someday."

"We'll do everything we can." A howl from outside made him whip his head around. "Wait here."

There was nothing else she could do. As Dad went to search the house, she sat in the dark and gazed down at the shotgun. Transient light from her TV box cast a red glow on the barrel. Point and shoot. All she had to do was sit here and point and shoot.

A tremor coursed down her spine. Fear spiked. She hadn't realized how afraid she felt until she was a sitting duck in the dark.

Rescue Rabbit. Drop the rescue and she was the scared rabbit ready to run.

Glass shattering echoed through the house. She gasped, clutching the hilt, but without knowing where she'd have to aim, she didn't move.

Grunts and wrestling came from the basement. Someone had gotten in through a bedroom window and was fighting Dad.

Please be all right. Please be all right.

Would she get in the way if she stood at the top and flipped the light on? Should she flip *all* the lights on? They could all see better than her.

Dammit, she didn't know what to do.

The front door burst open. Patience had the shotgun up and loosely aimed before she realized she was even standing. A tall male prowled inside. His skin was dirty and blood was smeared across his shoulders. Whose was it? He had shaggy hair and wasn't wearing a stitch of clothing. As he advanced, she was grateful for the dark. Not being able to see him clearly was less unnerving and she needed all the nerves she could get.

"Where is he?" a male growled as he advanced.

She was reasonably sure this wasn't her neighbor, Brenden. She swallowed. Resolve squared her shoulders. But she backed up as she asked, "Who?"

"That fucking brother of yours that thinks he can take one of our females."

Her brother had a shifter mate? That must've been why he was drawn to town.

The male kept advancing, his evil smile telling her that he enjoyed terrifying her.

"Stop or I'll shoot." Her voice shook.

He laughed, and behind him, another male appeared in the kitchen. The basement was quiet. Oh, God. "Dad?" she called.

She heard the male in the kitchen spit more than she could see him. "Fucking weak humans." Disgust rang in his voice.

The first male was close enough that he lifted an arm to bat the barrel of her gun away. She pulled the trigger. The blast muted all other sounds and she stumbled back, unable to recover herself and aim again. The male staggered back with his chest full of tiny holes. The second male pushed around him and rushed her.

She tried the trigger again, but he was faster. He batted the gun out of her hands and then gripped her, smacking her hard across the face.

"Time to teach you a lesson," he sneered, and pulled his fist back for another assault.

MALCOLM ROARED into the living room. He stomped on some bastard on the floor as he plowed through the room to get to Patience. Another male towered over her and blocked her completely, his arms flying as he attacked her. Malcolm ripped the male away and slammed him into the wall as he did. The male didn't have a chance to rebound, Malcolm was on him, fists flying, canines shredding any flesh that got near his mouth.

But the asshole shifted and it was fangs and claws.

Malcolm kicked the muzzle away from his leg. It'd take too long to undress. He'd have to do this with his hands.

A shotgun blast tore through his eardrums. The wolf yelped and dropped.

Malcolm frantically looked around. Patience stood to the side, the end of the shotgun lowered to the floor. "Are you hurt?" she asked.

"Are *you* hurt?"

The smell of her blood hung in the air, heavy and forlorn. The room fell quiet and she swayed to the side. Several cuts lined her arms, but there was a nasty gash oozing blood at her neck. "Did I kill him?"

"I don't know." He crossed to her, wrapping his arm around her and lending her his strength. "Is that the shotgun with the silver-laced ammo?"

She lifted a shoulder but leaned heavily on him. "How would I know?" She straightened with a gasp. "Dad!"

Shit. If anything happened to her father... He ignored the snarls and howls that came from the battle playing out in the yard. Wolves had been scattered over the lawn, chickens were squawking and Dot was going to give herself a goat heart attack if she didn't settle down. The dogs and cats thankfully stayed in the barn, too terrified to join in the melee. "Where is he?"

"The basement."

Before he went down there and dragged her with him because he wasn't leaving her side again, he ripped a piece of his shirt off and wrapped it around her neck. The amount of blood on her shirt concerned him. He swooped her into his arms and rushed down the stairs.

Paul Montgomery looked like he'd been tossed across the room and landed upside down on the couch. Dark blood puddled around his head, but his chest rose and fell.

"Dad!" She struggled to get out of his arms, but he held tight.

"He'll recover." It'd take time and he'd need a lot of red meat to replenish himself, but he was a shifter mate. He'd heal. Patience, on the other hand, might not. The cloth he'd put around her was already soaked. "We need to get you to a hospital."

"But—"

Malcolm had already spun around and was taking the stairs two at a time. He hoped Jacob was still behind the wheel. "Your wound is serious. Your dad is healing as we speak." As much as he wanted to stop and put Paul in a better position to recover, he couldn't. Patience was soaked in her own life source and fading in his arms. Her head dropped against his shoulder. Her lush, curvy body could just as well be disintegrating in his arms.

He crashed out the door. Wolves were down and ones he recognized prowled around them. Several shifters' coppery scents lingered in the air, their blood soaking into the dried grass. He didn't know how they'd clean this mess up and deal with intruders without outright killing them, but that wasn't his problem, either.

"Jacob! Where's Jacob?" He raced to the car. The driver's seat was empty. Fuck. "I need the keys."

A tawny wolf stretched into Tamera. "You'll never make it. Rescue Rabbit's lost too much blood. Her shirt is soaked." For once, Tamera's tone wasn't mocking.

"I have to try," he croaked, a part of him knowing she was right. Patience was limp and the blood kept coming. That bastard had nicked an artery and her sky-high heart rate had pumped the blood right out.

Tamera put her hands on her hips. "Or you could mate her."

"I don't...I can't..." He hadn't even had a chance to mark her as his yet. She wouldn't have a choice. Wasn't that what she fought against in her work? "I don't have a gladdus." The ceremonial dagger was critical to mating them. He'd tossed his when Tamera mated Darius.

"You can use ours." Brenden was in his human form and Delia was still in her wolf form, running to her house, presumably to get the dagger.

"She wouldn't know..." He didn't want to argue, but he had to do what was best for Patience.

"She would know she didn't die." Tamera didn't budge. "You know why I was so mean to her?" He clung to the woman who'd captured his heart as soon as he'd opened his bloodshot eyes that day and shook his head. "Because I could tell she was right for you. The curse of my special ability."

The admission left shock waves rippling through him. "What? Why didn't you mention anything?"

"Because nature needs to be allowed to take its course and too many of us have meddled with it. If you two found each other, and if you couldn't stand each other, then it wasn't meant to be." She rolled her shoulders and looked properly chagrined. "Didn't mean I had to like her for it."

"Do you think she'll hate me for this?"

"She'll be alive to hate you," she replied.

He looked at his brother who was still a chocolate brown wolf. Harrison dipped his brawny head. *The rest of us will keep these bastards down. Save your mate.*

Malcolm carefully laid her in an unbloodied part of the lawn. Delia charged around the house, the dagger in her mouth. Brenden grabbed it and, surrounded by shifters he'd known all his life and some he'd just met, Malcolm knelt next to the woman he could finally admit to falling in love with.

A commotion at the front door sounded and Paul staggered out. His gaze met Millie's where she stood by the barn before he flew to where Malcolm was with the man's daughter. "Can you save her?"

"She'll be my mate." But everything else would be by her choosing once she woke.

Brenden walked them through the ceremony. Malcolm hated gripping the blade with Patience's limp hand and slicing her tender flesh after she'd endured so much, but the deed was done.

He'd expected some fairy tale moment. A fluttering of the eyelids, followed by either a look of sheer love and appreciation or hate and derision. But she didn't move. He planted himself on his ass and gathered her into his arms and waited.

CHAPTER 19

This isn't right at all. Patience glowered at the mess in the basement.

Strong hands came around her waist and she broke into a smile, leaning back into the wall of muscle. "They boycotted the litter box and shit everywhere."

"I think they're ready for their fur-ever homes."

She nodded and ignored the mess in her spare bedroom. It'd been a couple months since the night of the massive attack, and she was happily mated. When she first woke to Malcolm's distraught gaze and profuse apologies, she made him promise to properly mark her like his kind did.

The memory of him actually doing it still made her body tingle weeks later.

"They're about ten weeks old now, so yes, I guess I could part with them. Another few weeks and they'll claw the paneling off the walls."

She knew they were about ten weeks old because she remembered the day she found them. After Malcolm had saved her, she woke up to her memory unlocking with each thought. The natural healing properties that came with being a shifter's mate had healed her mind. Jacob's too, since he and Rainey didn't wait more than a few days to tie their knot. Or slice their hands as it were.

"The paneling could use a good clawing. And don't worry, bunny. I'll clean it up."

It wasn't the first time she thought she was the luckiest woman alive. "We can take the mama cat to your brother's this weekend. And they wanted one more kitten. Apparently, their mountain lion friend isn't a mouser."

Her mate smirked. "Nala most definitely is not."

"Do we have to tell Brenden and Delia where we're going?"

Malcolm gave her a *what in the world are you talking about look*, then understanding dawned. "Ah, no. Not unless you want to."

She wasn't used to this pack stuff. Technically, she and Malcolm belonged to his pack of Guardians, but since his commander had conveniently stationed him here so he and Harrison could cover a large territory without having to travel back and forth as often, they functioned under the new pack established in Twin Forks. It was one of the concessions the shifters had to make after the Synod passed their ruling outlawing forced matings and imprisonment of a shifter who wanted to change locations. Those shifters had to belong to a pack. Their kind could not risk any instability. Brenden and Delia had been unofficial leaders for so long, most looked to them anyway.

Eventually, she and Malcolm would have to move. Same with Jacob and Rainey. They wouldn't age like the human population of their hometown thought they would. So they'd do like Tamera did and quietly move on. Last Patience heard, Tamera was loving the single life out of hiding.

Patience was sure that she and Malcolm would move to be closer to Harrison and she was fine with that. She talked to Sylva every week anyway and messaged her constantly. Same with Rainey, who delighted in all the treasures found in the garage. She was refurbishing Grandma's dolls and selling them for a mint. Grandma would be proud to see her loved trinkets getting new lives, along with Jacob and Patience.

She ran upstairs, planning to grab a few supplies and help Malcolm clean kitten shit that looked too large to come from such small bodies, when a knock on the door derailed her.

It was a gorgeous summer day and the front door was open, a soft breeze drifting in through the screen door. On the other side of the door stood a female that looked similar in age, but her eyes spoke of several years of life experience.

"Hi. Can I help you?" Patience never got lost people out here, and shifters didn't get lost. She didn't open the door but estimated how fast she could grab her trusty shotgun.

The smell of cigarette smoke wafted through the place. The female took a long drag before pinching the end off with her fingertips. There was something familiar about her. In the amber eyes and thick, dark hair secured in a long braid. She wore cheap jeans and an even cheaper T-shirt.

Blowing smoke out of the corner of her mouth, she eyed Patience. "You the human that plugged a few assholes full of silver?"

A spike of fear overwhelmed her. Had more escaped the Synod's punishment and come for her to finish the job? It'd be so much harder to kill her now, but this female looked capable of it. Patience really wanted to keep her head on her shoulders.

Footsteps pounded up the stairs and Malcolm tore around the corner. He skidded to a stop when he saw who was at the door. "Maw?"

That was it. She resembled a worn and world-weary version of Millie.

"Boy." She smacked her lips and sniffed, clearly uncomfortable, both with the confrontation and the emotions it was bringing up. "Been talking to Camille. Millie. Whatever the fuck she wants to be called."

Malcolm came to stand next to Patience. She squeezed his hand to let him know he had her support no matter what. She'd tell her—whatever you call a shifter mother-in-law—to take a hike if that's what he needed.

"And Harrison's been out to visit once," Maw continued. "But I gather you won't cuz your mate is human and all."

"I know how you feel," Malcolm said steadily. "And I won't subject Patience to that attitude."

Maw shifted her weight and shoved her hand in her back pocket. "Yeah, well, I guess times are changing. If she can drop two shifters, I guess I can reconsider." Her jaw tensed and moisture misted over her eyes. "I thought I lost one kid. I'm not keen to lose another."

Malcolm's grip tightened on hers. Thanks to their bond, she felt the emotion welling inside. Shock. Relief. Staggering love. Tentative joy.

"Come on in, Maw."

Maw jerked her thumb over her shoulder. "I gotta get your father."

"Father's with you?" Malcolm's voice rocked with disbelief.

Maw scoffed. "Why wouldn't he be?" was her reply before she marched off the porch to grab him.

"I can't fucking believe it," Malcolm muttered. "I mean, I knew he could leave whenever he wanted, but..."

"Maybe it's their version of separate beds." His parents had their own harrowing story. This was them on the calm side of it.

He chuckled softly and turned her to face him. Voices bickering with each other filtered into the house, but he ignored it and cupped her face. "You saved more than me that night. You saved my whole family."

And he kissed her the way she knew he'd kiss her for the rest of their lives.

MALCOLM AND HARRISON make their first appearance in the book that kicked this whole shifter world off. Fever Claim available for FREE on all retailers.

I'D LOVE to know what you thought of A Shifter's Salvation. Please consider leaving a review. Two words or two hundred, it all helps.

FOR ALL THE LATEST NEWS, sneak peeks, quarterly short stories, and free material sign up for my newsletter.

ABOUT THE AUTHOR

Marie Johnston lives in the upper-Midwest with her husband, four kids, and a lot of cats. Deciding to trade in her lab coat for a laptop, she's writing down all the tales she's been making up in her head for years. An avid reader of paranormal romance, these are the stories hanging out and waiting to be told between the demands of work, home, and the endless chauffeuring that comes with children.

ALSO BY MARIE JOHNSTON

Pale Moonlight:

Birthright (Book 1)

Ancient Ties (Book 2)

A Shifter's Second Chance (Book 3)

A Shifter's Claim (Book 4)

A Shifter's Bodyguard (Book 5)

A Shifter's Salvation (Book 6)

Printed in Great Britain
by Amazon